RED RIDING HOOD

a novel by **Sarah Blakley-Cartwright**

based on a screenplay written by **David Leslie Johnson**

introduction by Catherine Hardwicke

poppy

Little, Brown and Company
New York   Boston

To Catherine, Lauren, Laurie, and Ronee,
four incredible women

Introduction

IN AUGUST 2009, I was sent a script called *The Girl with the Red Riding Hood*, written by David Leslie Johnson and based on an idea by Leonardo DiCaprio. DiCaprio's company, Appian Way, had been developing the project with Warner Bros. I immediately fell in love with the idea of making a new, dark, layered version of the classic story.

Fairy tales are rich blueprints that help us understand and create our own worlds, which is exactly what I attempted to do with this one. My head was filled with images and ideas about how to make this world come alive. For inspiration, I pulled from creative sources all around me—my sister's paintings for the magic and the mood, current fashion runways for the clothes, a little northern

Russian architecture book I'd been saving since I was a teenager for the design of Daggorhorn.

In this version of "Red Riding Hood," I was interested in the modern feel of the characters and their relationships. The story explores themes of teenage angst and the pitfalls of growing up and falling in love. And, of course, there is the Big Bad Wolf. The Wolf in our story represents a dark, dangerous side of man and fosters a paranoid society.

This social paranoia stuck with me during the development of the script, and eventually it was built into the DNA of Daggorhorn's architecture. The villagers live in cottages that feel like miniature fortresses—they are elevated on stilts and have heavy wooden shutters and ladders that are pulled up at night. The people of the village are just as guarded emotionally as they are physically, and when their decades-long peace with the Wolf starts to break down, so do the ties among them.

The deeper we went into the world, the more I realized that the characters and their backstories were too complex to fit into the film, so I wanted to help create a novel to fully explore the tangled web of emotions in the village of Daggorhorn.

While on a trip to New York, I saw my friend Sarah Blakley-Cartwright. She had just graduated with honors from Barnard College with a degree in creative writing. I've known Sarah since she was thirteen—she'd even played small parts in all four of my previous films. She's always had an original, poetic spirit — full of whimsy — and I realized she would be perfect for this project.

From the moment I mentioned the idea to Sarah, she dove in headfirst. She flew to Vancouver, British Columbia, when we were building the sets for the movie, and she completely immersed herself in the world of *Red Riding Hood*. She interviewed all the actors about their characters, she participated in rehearsals, and she danced across hot coals in the festival scene. Sarah really became a part of the storytelling process.

I feel that Sarah has written a beautiful novel that has deepened the world of the characters. She allows us all to linger in the emotional moments, the ones that tell us that *Red Riding Hood* is not just a fairy tale, but rather a universal story about love and courage and growing up.

Enjoy.

—Catherine Hardwicke

Once upon a time . . .

. . . there was a Girl,

and there was a wolf.

Part One

1

From the towering heights of the tree, the little girl could see everything. The sleepy village of Daggorhorn lay low in the bowl of the valley. From above, it looked like a faraway, foreign land. A place she knew nothing about, a place without spikes or barbs, a place where fear did not hover like an anxious parent.

Being this far up in the air made Valerie feel as if she could be someone else, too. She could be an animal: a hawk, chilly with self-survival, arrogant and apart.

Even at age seven, she knew that, somehow, she was different from the other villagers. She couldn't help keeping them at a distance, even her friends, who were open and wonderful. Her older sister, Lucie, was the one person in the world to whom Valerie felt connected. She and Lucie were like the two vines that grew twisted together in the old song the elders of the village sang.

Lucie was the only one.

Valerie peered past her dangling bare feet and thought about why she had climbed up here. She wasn't allowed to, of course, but that wasn't it. And it wasn't for the challenge of the climb, either—that had lost its thrill a year earlier, when she first reached the tallest branch and found nowhere left to go but the open sky.

She climbed up high because she couldn't breathe down there, in the town. If she didn't get out, the unhappiness would settle upon her, piling up like snow until she was buried beneath it. Up here in her tree, the air was cool on her face and she felt invincible. She never worried about falling; such a thing was not possible in this weightless universe.

"Valerie!"

Suzette's voice sounded upward through the leaves, calling for her like a hand tugging Valerie back down to earth.

By the tone of her mother's voice, Valerie knew it was time to go. Valerie pulled her knees up under her, rose to a crouch, and began her descent. Looking straight down, she could see the steeply pitched roof of Grandmother's house, built right into the branches of the tree and covered in a thick shag of pine needles. The house was wedged in a flowering of branches as if it had lodged there during a storm. Valerie always wondered how it had gotten there,

4

but she never asked, because something so wonderful should never be explained.

It was nearing winter, and the leaves had begun to loosen themselves from their branches, easing their autumn grasp. Some shuddered and fell free as Valerie moved down the tree. She had perched in the tree all afternoon, listening to the low murmur of women's voices wafting up from below. It seemed like they were more cautious today, huskier than usual, as though the women were keeping secrets.

Nearing the lower branches that grazed the tree house roof, Valerie saw Grandmother float out onto the porch, her feet not visible beneath her dress. Grandmother was the most beautiful woman Valerie knew. She wore long layered skirts that swayed as she walked. If her right foot went forward, her silk skirt breezed to the left. Her ankles were delicate and lovely, like the tiny wooden dancer's in Lucie's jewelry box. This both delighted and frightened Valerie, because they looked like they could snap.

Valerie, herself unsnappable, leapt off the lowest branch and onto the porch with a solid thump.

She was not excitable like other girls, whose cheeks were pink or round. Valerie's were smooth and even and pale white. Valerie didn't really think of herself as pretty, or think about what she looked like, for that matter. No one else, though, could forget the corn-husk blonde with unsettling green eyes that lit up like they were charged by lightning. Her eyes, that knowing look she had, made her seem older than she was.

"Girls, come on!" her mother called from inside the house, anxiety bristling through her voice. "We need to be back early tonight." Valerie made it down before anyone could see that she had been in the tree at all.

Through the open door, Valerie saw Lucie bustle over to their mother clutching a doll she had dressed in scraps that Grandmother had donated to the cause. Valerie wished she could be more like her sister.

Lucie's hands were soft and round, a little bit pillowy, something Valerie admired. Her own hands were knobby and thin, tough with calluses. Her body was all angles. She felt deep inside that this made her unlovable, someone no one would want to touch.

Her older sister was better than she was, that much Valerie knew. Lucie was kinder, more generous, more patient. She never would have climbed above the tree house, where she knew sensible people didn't belong.

"Girls! It's a full moon tonight." Her mother's voice carried out to her now. "And it's our turn," she added sadly, her voice trailing off.

Valerie didn't know what to make of it being their turn. She hoped it was a surprise, maybe a present.

Looking down to the ground, she saw some markings in the dirt that formed the shape of an arrow.

Peter.

Her eyes widening, she headed down the steep, dusty stairs from the tree house to examine the marks.

No, it isn't Peter, she thought, seeing that they were just random scratches in the soil.

But what if—?

The marks stretched away from her into the woods. Instinctively, ignoring what she *should* do, what Lucie would do, she followed them.

Of course, they led nowhere. Within a dozen paces, the marks disappeared. Mad at herself for wishful thinking, she was glad that no one had seen her following nothing to nothing.

Before he'd left, Peter used to leave messages for her by drawing arrows in the dirt with the tip of a stick; the arrows guided her to him, often hiding deep in the woods.

He had been gone for months now, her friend. They had been inseparable, and Valerie still couldn't accept the fact that he wasn't coming back. His leaving had been like snipping off the end of a rope—leaving two unraveling strands.

Peter hadn't been like other boys, who teased and fought. He understood Valerie's impulses. He understood adventure; he understood not following the rules. He never judged her for being a girl.

"Valerie!" Grandmother's voice now called. Her calls were to be answered more urgently than Valerie's mother's because her threats might actually be carried out. Valerie turned from the puzzle pieces that had led to no prize, and hurried back.

"Down here, Grandmother." She leaned against the base

of the tree, delighting in the feel of the sandpaper bark. She closed her eyes to feel it fully — and heard the grumbling of wagon wheels like an approaching thunderstorm.

Hearing it, too, Grandmother slipped down the stairs to the forest floor. She wrapped Valerie in her arms, the cool silk of her blouse and the clunky jumble of her amulets pressing against Valerie's face. Her chin on Grandmother's shoulder, Valerie saw Lucie moving cautiously down the tall stairs, followed by their mother.

"Be strong tonight, my darlings," Grandmother whispered. Held tightly, Valerie stayed quiet, unable to voice her confusion. For Valerie, each person and place had its own scent — sometimes, the whole world seemed like a garden. She decided that her grandmother smelled like crushed leaves mingled with something deeper, something profound that she could not place.

As soon as Grandmother released Valerie, Lucie handed her sister a bouquet of herbs and flowers she'd gathered from the woods.

The wagon, pulled by two muscular workhorses, came bumping over the ruts in the road. The woodcutters were seated in clusters atop freshly chopped tree stumps that slid forward as the wagon lurched to a stop in front of Grandmother's tree. Branches — the fattest ones at the bottom and the lightest on top — were piled between the men. To Valerie, the riders looked like they were made of wood themselves.

Valerie saw her father, Cesaire, seated near the back of

the cart. He stood and reached down for Lucie. He knew better than to try for Valerie. He reeked of sweat and ale, and she stayed far away from him.

"I love you, Grandmother!" Lucie called over her shoulder as she let Cesaire help her and her mother over the side of the cart. Valerie scrambled up and in on her own. With a snap of the reins, the wagon lumbered to a start.

A woodcutter shifted aside to give Suzette and the girls room, and Cesaire reached over, landing a theatrical kiss on the man's cheek.

"Cesaire," Suzette hissed, casting him a quietly reproachful glance as side conversations picked up in the wagon. "I'm surprised you're still conscious at this late hour."

Valerie had heard accusations like this before, always veiled behind a false overtone of cleverness or wit. And yet it still jolted her to hear them said with such a tone of contempt.

She looked at her sister, who hadn't heard their mother because she was laughing at something another woodcutter had said. Lucie always insisted that their parents were in love, that love was not about grand gestures but rather about the day to day, about being there, going to work and coming home in the evening. Valerie had tried to believe that this was true, but she couldn't help feeling that there had to be something more to love, something less practical.

Now she hung on tight as she leaned over the back rails of the wagon, peering down at the rapidly disappearing ground. Feeling dizzy, she turned to face back in.

"My baby." Suzette pulled Valerie onto her lap, and Valerie let her. Her pale, pretty mother smelled like almonds and powdery flour.

As the wagon emerged from the Black Raven Woods and rumbled alongside the silver river, the dreary haze of the village came into full view. Its foreboding was palpable even at a distance: Stilts, spikes, and barbs jutted up and out. The granary's lookout tower, the town's tallest point, stretched high.

It was the first thing one felt while coming over the ridge: *fear.*

Daggorhorn was a town full of people who were afraid, people who felt unsafe even in their beds and vulnerable with each step, exposed with every turn.

The people had begun to believe that they deserved the torture—that they had done something wrong and that something inside them was bad.

Valerie had watched the villagers cowering in fear every day and felt her difference from them. What she feared more than the outside was a darkness that came from inside her. It seemed as if she was the only one who felt that way.

Other than Peter, that is.

She thought back to when he'd been there, the two of them fearless together and filled with reckless joy. Now she resented the villagers for their fear, for the loss of her friend.

Once through the massive wooden gates, the town looked like any other in the kingdom. The horses kicked up pockets of dust as they did in all such towns, and every face was familiar. Stray dogs roamed the streets, their bellies empty and drooping, sucked in impossibly tight at the sides so that their fur looked striped. Ladders rested gently against porches. Moss spilled out from crevices in roofs and crawled across the fronts of houses, and no one did anything about it.

Tonight, the villagers were hurrying to bring their animals inside.

It was Wolf night, just as it had been every full moon for as long as anyone could remember.

Sheep were herded and locked behind heavy doors. Handed off from one family member to another, chickens strained their necks as they were thrust up ladders, stretching them out so far that Valerie worried they would rip them clean off their own bodies.

As they reached home, Valerie's parents spoke to each other in low voices. Instead of climbing up the ladder to their raised cottage, Cesaire and Suzette approached the stable underneath, which was darkened by the shady gloom of their house. The girls ran ahead of them to greet Flora, their pet goat. Seeing them, she clattered her hooves against the rickety boards of the pen, her clear eyes watery with anticipation.

"It's time now," Valerie's father said, coming up behind Valerie and Lucie and laying his hands on their shoulders.

"Time for what?" Lucie asked.

"It's our turn."

Valerie saw something in his stance that she didn't like, something menacing, and she backed away from him. Lucie reached for Valerie's hand, steadying her as she always did.

A man who believed in speaking truthfully to his children, Cesaire plucked at the fabric of his pants and bent down to have a word with his two little girls. He told them that Flora was to be this month's sacrifice.

"The chickens provide us with eggs," he reminded them. "The goat is all we can afford to offer."

Valerie stood in stupefied disbelief. Lucie knelt down sorrowfully, scratching her little fingernails up and down the goat's neck and pulling softly at her ears in the way that animals will only allow children to do. Flora nudged Lucie's palm with her newly sprouted horns, trying them out.

Suzette glanced at the goat and then looked at Valerie expectantly.

"Say good-bye, Valerie," she said, resting her hand on her daughter's slender arm.

But Valerie couldn't—something held her back.

"Valerie?" Lucie looked at her imploringly.

She knew her mother and sister thought she was being cold. Only her father understood, nodding at her as he led the goat away. He steered Flora by a thin rope, her nostrils flaring and her eyes sharp with unease. Holding back bitter tears, Valerie hated her father, for his sympathy and for his betrayal.

Valerie was careful, though. She never let anyone see her cry.

That night, Valerie lay awake after her mother had put them to bed. The glow of the moon streamed through her window, stretching across the floorboards in one great pillar.

She thought hard. Her father had taken Flora, their precious goat. Valerie had seen Flora birthed on the floor of the stable, the mother goat bleating in pain as Cesaire brought the small, damp kid forth into the world.

She knew what she had to do.

Lucie padded along beside Valerie, leaving the warmth of their bed and heading down the loft ladder and to the front door.

"We've got to do something!" Valerie whispered urgently, beckoning for her sister to join her.

But Lucie stayed back, fearful, shaking her head and wordlessly willing Valerie to stay, too. Valerie knew that she couldn't do as her elder sister did, huddling in the doorway, clutching her doe hide. She would not just stand by and watch the events of her life unfold. But just as Lucie had always admired Valerie's commitment, Valerie admired her sister's restraint.

Valerie wanted to cover up her uneasy sister now and tell her not to worry, to say, "Shhhh, sweet Lucie, everything will be all right by morning." Instead, she turned, holding down the latch of the door with her thumb and letting it ease noiselessly into the jamb before she plunged into the cold.

The village was especially sinister that night, backlit by the brightness of the moon, the color of shells that had been bleached by the sun. The houses hulked like tall ships, and the branches of the trees jutted out like barbed masts against the night sky. As Valerie set out for the first time on her own, she felt like she was discovering a new world.

To reach the altar more quickly, Valerie took a shortcut through the woods. She stepped through the moss, which had the texture of bread soaked through with milk, and avoided the mushrooms, white blisters whose tops were speckled with brown, as if dusted with cinnamon.

Something pulled at her out of the dark, clinging to her cheek like wet silk. A spider's web. It felt like her entire body was crawling with invisible insects. She tore at her face, trying to brush off the filmy web, but the strands were too thin, and there was nothing to hold on to.

The full moon hung lifeless overhead.

Once she reached the clearing, her steps became more cautious. She felt queasy as she walked, the same feeling she got while cleaning a sharp knife—the feeling that one small slip could be disastrous. The villagers had dug a sinkhole trap into the soil, staked sharpened wooden rods into the ditch, and covered them with a false ground of grass. Valerie knew that the hole was somewhere near, but she had always been led safely around it. Now, even though she thought she'd passed it, she wasn't entirely sure.

A familiar bleating pulled her on, though, and there ahead she could see Flora, pathetic and alone, stumbling in the wind and crying out. Valerie began to run toward the goat's sad form struggling alone in the bone-white moonlit clearing. Seeing Valerie, Flora reared up wildly and craned her slender neck in Valerie's direction as much as her rope would allow.

"I'm here, I'm here," Valerie began to call out, but the words died in her throat.

She heard something bounding furiously over a great length at a quick pace, coming closer and closer still through the darkness. Valerie's feet refused to move, much as she tried to continue.

In a moment, everything went still again.

And it appeared.

At first, just a streak of black. Then the Wolf was there, facing away from her, its back massive and monstrous, its tail moving seductively back and forth, tracing a pattern in the dust. It was so big that she could not see it all at once.

Valerie's breath burst out in a gasp, jagged with fear. The Wolf's ears froze, then quivered, and it turned its eyes to meet hers.

Eyes that were savage and beautiful.

Eyes that *saw* her.

Not an ordinary kind of seeing, but seeing in a way that no one had seen her before. Its eyes penetrated her, recognizing something. The terror hit her then. She crumpled to the ground, unable to look any longer, and burrowed deep into the refuge of darkness.

A great shadow loomed over her. She was so small and it was so immense that she felt the cover of the standing figure weigh down upon her as though her body were sinking into the ground. A shiver coursed through her body as it responded to the threat. She imagined the Wolf tearing through her flesh with its hooked canines.

There was a roar.

Valerie waited to feel the leap, to feel the snap of its jaws and the ripping of claws, but she felt nothing. She heard a scuffling and a tinkling of Flora's bells, and it was only then that she realized the shape had lifted. From her crouch, she heard gnashing and gnarling. But there was something else, another sound that she couldn't identify. Much later, she would learn that it was the roar of a dark rage being let loose.

Then there followed a panicked silence, a frenetic calm. Finally, she couldn't resist slowly lifting her head to look for Flora.

All was still.

Nothing was left but the broken tether still tied to the stake, lying slack on the dusty ground.

V alerie sat waiting at the edge of the road with her legs outstretched, the ground damp with early morning dew. She didn't worry about her feet getting run over; she never worried about things like that. She was older now — ten years had passed since the awful night when she had looked into the eyes of evil. Walking past the sacrificial altar today, though, Valerie hadn't even noticed the pile of bones left over from the previous night's offering. Like all the other children in the village, she'd seen it once a month all her life and stopped thinking about what it meant.

Most children became obsessed with full-moon nights at some point in their lives, stopping at the altar the following mornings to examine the dried blood and asking questions: *Does the Wolf talk? Is it like the other wolves in the forest? Why is the Wolf so bad?* The answers they were given were often more frustrating than none at all. Parents tried to protect the children, shushing them, telling them not to talk about it. But sometimes they let slip some information, saying, "We put a sacrifice here so that the Wolf doesn't come and eat up cute little girls like you," while nipping their noses.

Ever since her encounter with the Wolf, Valerie had stopped asking about it. Often at night, though, she would become overwhelmed by the memory. She would wake up and watch Lucie, an easy sleeper, lying much too still in their shared bed. Feeling desperately alone, Valerie would gaze at her sister for a long time until the panic became too much, and she would reach up to feel Lucie's heartbeat.

"Stop it!" Lucie would slur sleepily, reaching up and swatting at Valerie's hand. Valerie knew that her sister didn't like to think of her heartbeat. It reminded her that she was alive, that she was fallible, just flesh and bones.

Now Valerie ran her fingers over the chilled ground of the walkway, feeling the grooves between the hunks of old sandstone. The stone felt like it might collapse, like it was rotting from the inside and, with just a little more time, she would be able to crumble off bits with her fingers. The leaves of the trees were yellow, as though they had absorbed all the spring sunshine and were saving it for winter.

It was easier to shrug off last night's full moon on a day like today. The whole village was in a commotion as everyone prepared for the harvest: Men ran with rusty scythes, and women leaned out of their cottage windows, dropping loaves of bread into passing baskets.

Soon Valerie saw Lucie's broad, beautiful face as her sister came up the walk on the way back from taking a broken latch to the blacksmith for repair. As Lucie came up the path, some of the villagers' young daughters trailed behind her doing a strange, ritualistic walk. As they came closer, Valerie realized that Lucie was teaching the four little girls how to curtsy.

Lucie was soft in a way that no one else was, a softness of nature and being. Her hair was not red or blond; it was both. She didn't belong here in Daggorhorn; she belonged in a cottony land where the skies were marbled yellow, blue, and pink, like watercolors. She spoke in poetry, her voice sweet like a song. Valerie felt as if her family were just borrowing Lucie.

How strange it is to have a sister, Valerie thought. *Someone you might have been.*

Lucie stopped in front of Valerie, and the train of girls stopped, too. A small one with dirt-stained knees looked at Valerie judgmentally, disappointed in her for not being more like her older sister. The village had always thought of Valerie as the other one, the more mysterious sister, the not-Lucie. Two of the girls studied a man across the road who was frantically trying to yoke his ox to his wagon.

"Hi!" Lucie twirled the fourth young girl around, bending down to hold the girl's small hand above her head. The girl was hesitant to make the turn, to look away from her idol. The other girls looked impatient, feeling as if they, too, should be included.

Valerie scratched her leg, peeling at a scab.

Lucie stayed her sister's hand. "It'll scar." Lucie's legs were unblemished, flawless. She moisturized them with a concoction of wheat flour and oil when there was extra to be had.

Examining her own legs—bug-bitten, bruised, and picked at—Valerie asked, "Have you heard anything about the campout?"

Lucie leaned in. "Everyone else has permission!" she whispered. "Now we *have* to go."

"Well, now it comes down to convincing Mother."

"You try."

"Are you mad? She'll never say yes to me. You're the one who always gets whatever it is you want."

"Maybe." Lucie's lips were big and pink. When she was nervous, she chewed them pinker. "Maybe you're right," she said, grinning. "In any case, I'm a step ahead of you."

With a sly smile, she held her basket out to Valerie, who guessed what was inside before she saw. Or maybe she'd smelled them. Their mother's favorite sweet cakes.

"*Such* a good idea!" Valerie stood, brushing the dirt off the back of her tunic.

Lucie, pleased with her foresight, put her arm around Valerie. Together, they returned the little girls to their mothers, who were working in the gardens. Women were tough in this village, and yet even the gruffest among them smiled up at Lucie.

Heading home, they passed a few pigs wheezing like sick old men, a baby goat that tried to tag along with some disdainful chickens, and a serene cow munching on hay.

They passed the long row of houses, standing on their stilts as if ready to wander away, and arrived at the second one from the end. Hoisting themselves up the ladder, the girls entered the landscape of their lives. The wood dresser was so warped that the drawers refused to close. The wooden rope bed gave splinters. The washboard their father had made for their mother the winter before was worn down now — she needed another. The basket for berries was low and flat, to ensure that none got crushed. In a shaft of light from the window, a few bits of feather stuffing hung in the air, reminding Valerie of when they jumped on the mattress as girls and entire clouds of feathers would float around them.

There wasn't much to distinguish their home from the others. The furniture in Daggorhorn was simple and functional. Everything served a purpose. A table had four legs and a flat top, nothing more.

Their mother was home, of course. Working over the stove, she was lost in thought. Her hair was pulled into a loose bun at the top of her head, a few strands hanging free at the nape of her neck.

Before the girls came in, Suzette had been thinking of her husband, of all his faults and all his virtues. The fault that she blamed him for most of all—the fault that was not forgivable—was that he was unimaginative. She was thinking of a recent day. Feeling dreamy, feeling like giving him a chance, she'd asked hopefully: *What is outside the walls, do you think?* He'd chewed his food, swallowed. Even tossed back some ale. He'd looked like he was thinking. *A whole lot more of the same, I reckon.* Suzette had felt like falling to the ground.

People left her family alone. Suzette felt cut off from things, like a marionette whose strings had been snipped.

Stirring the stew, she realized she was caught in a whirlpool—the more she struggled to get out, the more vehemently she was dragged down, down, down....

"Mother!" Lucie came up behind her and gently tickled her back.

Suzette returned to the world of daughters and uncooked stew.

"Are you girls thirsty?" Suzette brightened, pouring out two cups of water. She sweetened Lucie's with a nip of honey, but Valerie, she knew, had no use for it. "You two have a big day today," she said, handing the appropriate glass to each girl.

Suzette was grateful that she had the excuse of staying

home to cook the men's harvest meal. She went back to stirring the stew in a huge round pot with handles on both sides. The pot had a low-seated belly that always made Lucie feel strange because it was not quite a half sphere. Lucie didn't like things that seemed incomplete. Valerie peered in. In the pot was a medley of brown oats and tan and gray seeds—some green peas stood out garishly.

Lucie chattered while Valerie set to work helping Suzette chop the spindly strands off the carrots. Suzette was silent. Lucie's talking filled the dead air, but Valerie wondered whether something was wrong. Waiting out her mother's mood, as she had learned to do in the past, she added some vegetables to the pot. Collards, garlic, onions, leeks, spinach, and parsley.

What Valerie could not know was that Suzette had returned to thoughts of her husband. Cesaire was a caring father, a supportive husband. But that was not all Suzette had promised herself. If expectations had been set lower, his failures might not have been so devastating.

For what he did do, for the end that he *had* held up, Suzette was grateful. For those things, she felt she had repaid him sufficiently by keeping a tidy household and by loving their children. She had to acknowledge that maybe in marriage, as in any contractual obligation, in matters of owing and being owed, there was no allowance for love.

Feeling satisfied with this conclusion, Suzette turned to

her girls to find Valerie gazing at her with those penetrating green eyes, almost as though she could hear her
mother's thoughts. Suzette didn't know where Valerie's
eyes had come from; both hers and Cesaire's were fawn
brown. She cleared her throat.

"Good that you girls are helping out like this. I've said it
before, and I'll say it again: You'll need to be able to cook,
Valerie, when you start to build your own home. Lucie
already knows."

Lucie was like Suzette. They foresaw and planned. Valerie and Cesaire were quick to think and quick to act.

"I'm *seventeen*. Let's not rush it." Valerie sliced a potato
through the skin and the dull velvety meat. She let the two
halves fall open and bobble on the uneven table. She didn't
like to think of the things her mother always insisted on
talking about.

"You are of marriageable age, Valerie. You're a young
woman now."

With this concession, all thoughts of any future responsi-
bility dissipated from the sisters' minds. They saw their
moment.

"So, Mother. We're leaving for the harvest soon," Lucie
began.

"Yes, of course. Your first time, Valerie," Suzette said,
looking down to conceal her pride. She had begun grating
cabbage.

"Some people, some women, are staying on afterward..."
Valerie added.

"...for the little campfire thing," Lucie continued.

"Mm-hmmm," Suzette allowed, her mind beginning to wander.

"Prudence's mother is taking some of the other girls to camp out..." said Valerie.

"...and we wanted to know if we could go," Lucie finished.

"With Prudence's mother?" Suzette processed the one piece of concrete information she'd been given.

"Yes," said Valerie.

She seemed to accept this explanation. "The other mothers already said yes?"

"Yes," Valerie said again.

"All right. I guess that would be okay," she said absentmindedly.

"Thank you, thank you, thank you!"

It was only then, seeing the extent of their gratitude, that Suzette realized she'd consented to something maybe she shouldn't have.

"I can't believe she said yes!" Valerie exclaimed.

"That was so good, how you kept saying yes, so she didn't have time to think about it!"

The girls ambled down the rutty road to the town square.

"And you were so good, tickling her back!"

"That was good, right? I know she likes it." Lucie smiled in satisfaction.

"Lucie! Don't tell me you brought your whole wardrobe." Their friend Roxanne peered at them from around the corner, her pale brow knit into lines of concern. Two more girls came into view behind her: Prudence and Rose.

Lucie was cradling her pack in her arms, and Valerie belatedly realized that it was bulging.

"You're going to have to carry it around all day," Valerie said.

Prudence scowled, knowing Lucie got overambitious sometimes. "We are *not* going to carry it for you if you get tired."

"Extra blankets." Lucie smiled. She got cold easily.

"Planning on having company?" Rose asked, one eyebrow arched.

Valerie thought their three friends looked like a trio of mythical goddesses. Roxanne's hair was rust-colored and smooth. It was so fine, it looked as though all of it could fit inside one stalk of straw. Her freckles were faint, like spots on a butterfly's wings. Between all her corsets and blouses and shawls, it was obvious to Valerie that she was shy about her body.

Rose, on the other hand, kept the ties of her blouse loose and didn't rush to fix it if it fell a little too low. She was pretty, with a heart-shaped mouth and a sharp face — she sucked her checks in to make it more so. Her hair was so dark that it was black or brown or blue, depending on the light. If you put her in a finer top, Rose could almost pass for a lady . . . at least until she opened her mouth.

Prudence was a melancholic beauty with light brown hair and a calculating manner. She was often too quick with a sharp word, but she usually apologized. She was tall and somewhat imperious.

All five girls headed out through the village gates and up the hill toward the field, falling in with the parade of men, who were excited, too. The town itself felt wide awake, the anticipation floating in the air like the smell of a strong, unexpected spice.

Roxanne's brother, Claude, caught up with them, stumbling as he tried to kick a stone forward with each step.

"H-h-hi." Claude's eyes were quick and gray. He was a bit younger than the girls, a village outcast who'd always been a little . . . *different.* Claude wore a single suede glove without explanation and was always shuffling a deck of homemade cards that he carried with him at all times. The pockets were forever pulled out of his patchwork pants, a mash-up of all the pieces of burlap and hide his mother had lying around. He was teased about them, but he didn't mind; he was proud of the incredible work by his mother, who stayed up late into the nights sewing, and who worked hard enough at the tavern as it was.

It was said that Claude had been dropped on his head as an infant, and that was why he was strange. Valerie thought that notion was ridiculous. He was a beautiful soul.

The trouble was that instead of rushing to get in his own

words as everyone else did, he really listened. And that made people think he was slow. But he was kind and good, a lover of animals and people.

He never washed his socks. And no one washed them for him, either.

Both he and Roxanne were freckled, but Claude more so, even on his lips.

Everyone called Roxanne and Claude redheads, but Valerie never knew why. She thought it must have been for lack of imagination. She would call them six-o'clock-in-the-evening-sunset-heads. Bottom-of-the-lake-tendrils-of-algae-heads. Valerie grew up feeling envious of those heads of hair because she felt they were something special, a mark from God.

Claude and Valerie listened as the other girls chattered about the boys from neighboring villages who would be coming to help with the harvest. Claude lost interest and ambled back toward the center of town.

Something changed in the air, though, as the girls passed a temporary outdoor blacksmith shop that had been set up on the path to the harvest. A sense of self-awareness set in. A quickening of breath. A loss of focus. Valerie narrowed her eyes in disappointment at her friends; they were too smart for this. Losing it over a boy. *Henry Lazar.*

He was lanky and dashing, with cropped hair and a relaxed smile. The girls saw him at work outside with his equally handsome father, Adrien, repairing axles for the harvest wagons. The way some people loved to cook or to work in the garden, Henry loved the intricacies of locks, the process of the planning, the designing, the making. He had shown a few he made to Valerie once, square and round, one shaped unwittingly like the head of a cat, another like an upturned house drawn by a child, or a family crest. Some black, some gold, some gold underneath blackened tarnish.

Valerie waved easily as her friends went mute, smiled shyly at their feet, and shuttled past. Only Lucie curtsied politely. Henry shook his head, grinning.

Rose hung back at the last moment to make very sure her eyes met Henry's and held his gaze long enough to make him feel uncomfortable.

Other than that, the girls pretended that Henry hadn't affected them at all, and self-consciously continued with their conversation. Close as they all were, they felt that admitting their attraction would make themselves vulnerable. Besides, this way, each girl got to feel as if she were keeping Henry to herself. Valerie couldn't help wondering why her own reaction was so different from theirs. True, he was good-looking, charming, tall, and kind, but he did not leave her feeling girly and giddy.

"I hope you guys haven't forgotten who's coming today," Valerie teased them.

"Some of them *have* to be handsome," Lucie jumped in. "By the rule of ratios."

The girls looked at one another and reached for each other's hands, jumping up and down in unison. They would be free for the night.

And in Daggorhorn, a night of freedom meant everything.

3

It was still so early that the morning light cast a hushed pink glow on the hay fields, and they looked almost too beautiful to be touched. Valerie and her friends watched as the first men out from the village hovered, not speaking. The men felt foolish, but no one wanted to be the first to hack into the even sheet of hay. Work was work, though, and so they set to it.

The men were just laying the first blows when they heard the rumbling of wheels. A wedding in the village a week earlier had made a big impression on Valerie's friends. Now the girls couldn't help but wonder whether the foreign wagons' cargo would change their lives. But the older men of the village, already hard at work, held a sad knowledge: No matter how good the boys were, they would never be able to live up to the girls' expectations.

The wagon lurched to a stop; the horse pulling it was so inky black that it looked like a silhouette against the light wheat background. As the guest laborers from other villages began to pour out, the girls rose from the haystacks where they sat, shaking out their skirts in preparation. The boys were energetic, young, and strong, and Valerie was happy for her friends, who were light-headed with excitement. Somehow, though, she knew there wouldn't be anyone for her — not among these village boys. They just lacked . . . *something.*

The men, stepping out, shaded their eyes against the sun. They carried blankets rolled into packs and jackets slung loose over their shoulders.

The younger ones' eyes scanned the girls. They knew this dance well. An especially eager harvester stopped in front of a stunned Roxanne, who held her breath, afraid to disrupt the air around her.

"Hi," he said, flashing all his teeth, trying hard.

He didn't see Prudence pinch Roxanne's thigh.

"Hello," Prudence said for her.

Lucie looked down, demure, while Rose scooted her breasts higher up into the corset of her blouse. Prudence's eyes flickered, darting from one boy to the next, weighing their cons (this one had the gangliest limbs) against their pros (but also the nicest leather bag). The choosing seemed a matter of utmost importance.

As soon as they had gone, the girls ran toward one another into a huddle, narrowly avoiding collision.

"So many!" Roxanne cried, blowing at a stray wisp of hair.

"Just the right amount." Prudence caught her breath, having singled out the good ones.

"One for each, with a few left over for me." Rose sashayed in her skirt.

"Valerie, are you sure you have the tea?" Lucie interrupted, putting a momentary halt to the excitement.

"Yes."

Lucie gave her a look, knowing her sister's forgetfulness.

"Yes, yes, I'm sure," Valerie said, patting her pack.

They resumed staking their claims without even considering that the boys might like to have a say in the matter. Prudence felt she deserved the harvester who'd come up to Roxanne, as she'd been the one to actually speak to him. Valerie thought it was a bit grabby, but Roxanne didn't argue, as she had her eye on a quieter, less forward one anyway.

Lucie pointed to a passing harvester, portly in his breeches.

"There goes your husband now, Rose!"

"At least I don't have a crush on a sheep shearer who could be my grandfather." Rose's angular face made her seem angry, even when she wasn't.

Roxanne felt compelled to mention the person missing at the scene. "Oh, who cares?" she said, smoothing a lock of her red hair. "Henry is better looking than all of them."

"You know he's not going to marry any of us village girls," Prudence snapped, as she sometimes did. "We're all too poor."

The girls saw the village authority and harvest overseer, the Reeve, coming toward them, so they trudged out to the fields and set to work, swaying on their slender legs as they raked the grass into rows for drying. Valerie wished she didn't feel so divorced from her friends' excitement—it must have been wonderful to feel dizzy with joy, as they did. Try as she might, love had never been a topic that had much interested her. Now Valerie felt the dejection one experienced after a holiday had come and gone.

Seeing Valerie's disinterest, Prudence was pleased. *More for me to choose from*, she thought, surveying the men in the fields. Just then, her eye caught another wagon coming in, so unexpected that she didn't even have a chance to meet her friends' eyes before its big wheels rolled to a stop. They saw, too, though. Lucie lifted her head but pretended to work, picking up and setting down the same small heap repeatedly. Rose blotted her face with the inside of her skirt, and Roxanne swiped at the hair clinging to her forehead, already sticky with sweat from the muggy air.

The horse slowed to a stop, the cart's wheels lurching forward one last time and then rocking back into a rut. Valerie watched as a few older men toddled out of the wagon, but then went back to work with her wide-toothed rake as the rest of the harvesters drifted out. She could sense her friends scrutinizing the new arrivals.

She wasn't sure what made her look up again—years later, remembering this morning as the one that forever altered the course of her life, she always said that she'd felt something out of the corner of her eye, compelling her to look, almost as if someone had tapped her on the shoulder to make her turn. Looking up, she saw a heart-stoppingly handsome, dark-haired young man.

He looked wild and haunted, wearing all black, like a horse that could not be tamed.

Valerie felt her breath empty out of her.

Peter and I had spent the day chasing each other around the fields, collecting huge white mushrooms, whose layered, dusty, charcoal bottoms were soft and crumbling. We'd collapsed upon reaching the square and begun playing a game of riddles, charades, something I was never good at. I became hopelessly lost, never able to keep track of whether we were on the third syllable or the second of the third word or the fifth, and, wait a moment, how many words were there in all?

But Peter's father appeared from out of nowhere and yanked him up, saying, "We need to leave. Now."

Shouts echoed behind him: "Con man! Scoundrel! Thief!"

Peter had looked back over his shoulder as his father dragged him away by a hand. Villagers gathered in a mob, waving weapons. An angry farmhand chased after them with a lit torch outstretched: "That's right, get out of here! And never come back."

They'd left town immediately, and it was the last Valerie

had seen of Peter. From the looks on the villagers' faces that day, she'd assumed he was dead.

But now...

I must be crazy, she thought. It had been ten years. She had given up; she had stopped searching for his arrows. He couldn't be the same person... *could he?*

Also seeing the boy, her friends eyed each other worriedly. He looked like no one else, like the purple glow at the base of a flame, the most beautiful and the most dangerous. He kept his head down as he made his way through the fields, his eyes locked on the ground. He avoided meeting the eyes of the villagers; clearly he answered to no one.

Seeing Valerie's transfixed gaze, Lucie tossed some hay into the air in front of her. But Valerie did not awake.

Valerie edged closer to the figure. *Is it him?* But the Reeve swooped in, pushing through a hefty patch of reeds, and instructed her to stay in her line. Valerie wondered fleetingly whether the Reeve suspected something, whether he had noticed the way she reacted, the way her skin had flushed and her eyes had softened, and was separating them purposefully. She felt shamed but regained her common sense. He would have no reason to. She was only curious, nostalgic for her childhood friend, for the fun they had once had together.

He was just a boy she'd played with, older now. *Right?*

The Reeve continued, barking an unbroken string of orders that, with time, came to sound like a narrative. She watched as the person who might be Peter set down his

40

bag, a worn piece of cloth, the opening drawn together with a piece of fraying string. He began to swing his massive scythe, brandishing it expertly across the grass. He glued his chin to his chest, burying his face in work.

Valerie tried to watch him, but the largest of the harvesters came between them, shirtless, his upper arms dimpled like cauliflower. When the monolithic harvester wasn't in the way, the Reeve was weaving between the rows. Valerie could only see the object of her attention in flashes. A hand gripping the handle of the rake...a smooth olive calf... the set of a jawbone. He was lashing with a rhythmic motion. Pounding. Sweating. Muscles working.

Finally, she caught a good angle. It *was* Peter. She was sure of it. Her heart clapped against her chest, even now, so many years later. Back then, it had been an innocent infatuation, something between children, but now...she felt something else.

Valerie thought back to when she and Peter used to lie on their stomachs, nestled into the sprawling roots of the Great Pine. Then they'd climb to the top to see all the other towns they would leave their village to visit one day.

Only Peter had actually gotten out.

Now Valerie longed to be near him, to know him again, to know whether he was still the same. She was lost in these thoughts, and her eyes were resting on him when he looked up. His gaze met hers through the hay-flecked air. He paused in the flow of his work, his brown eyes still and opaque. Then he looked away.

Did he not know her? Had he forgotten? Or perhaps he belonged to someone else....

Valerie's rake stilled in the air, suspended.

Should she go to him?

But, then, as though nothing had happened—*swoosh, swoosh, swoosh*—swinging his scythe hard and fast, Peter was back to his work. He did not look up again.

4

Valerie."

Kneeling on the ground, tying up a sheaf of the honey-tinted hay, she heard a strong male voice above her. *He remembers.* She was still, frozen, unable to look up.

"Valerie?"

She slowly raised her head—only to see Henry Lazar holding out a battered jug of water.

"Are you all right?"

"Yes."

"I thought maybe you'd gone deaf from working too hard." His dark brows were lifted into curves with the question.

"Oh. No," she stumbled, shaken.

She ignored the water and reached for the thick copper mallet he was holding in his other hand and lifted it to her cheek. The metal was deliciously cool.

She looked around, the movement of the harvest softened in the golden haze of dust. She tried to angle past Henry for a better view. The trouble was, though, that Henry followed, blocking Peter from sight.

Valerie felt her heat rush into the mallet, and soon it was no good anymore. As she handed it back, Henry squinted at her and laughed. Valerie put a hand to her cheek — it came away black. There was a round, soot-stained circle on each of her cheeks.

"You're like a tough-girl china doll."

In spite of herself, she liked how that sounded.

Valerie declined his handkerchief and wiped her face on her sleeve. She knew the water was only an excuse for Henry to be out in the fields, to be included in the day. He got left out of a lot of things because of his family's stature in the town; it was hard for him, she knew, to be in a class by himself. She looked down at his new leather boots, though, which were so shiny that they reflected, and she lost whatever sympathy she'd had for him. To buy boots like those when the people around him didn't have enough to eat seemed unfeeling.

"I know they're stupid," he said with a quiet smile. Valerie realized she hadn't been subtle. "Embarrassing. But they're a gift from my grandmother."

Still not okay, she thought, feeling belligerent. She tried to see if Peter had noticed her talking with Henry. But he seemed to have no interest; Valerie could tell he had not looked once.

Henry muttered that he needed to offer water to others. All the surrounding young women, who had neglected their work to watch Henry, quickly got back to binding the cut hay at their feet. As he continued down the line, though, Valerie could feel his eyes lingering on her, longer than they should have.

Henry knew Valerie was in one of her contrarian moods. She wanted to be alone. As he moved away, though, he couldn't help watching her. Rumors had circulated, rumors that she had seen the Wolf as a child, that it had changed her, and that she'd never been the same. When anyone asked, she wouldn't tell. But it was a small town, and there were no secrets.

He'd always known she was different, but he'd always felt a little different himself. Henry thought maybe they could be different together.

The midday sun blazed down from the center of the sky. It had baked the fields so that they smelled burned. Sheltered from the cruel heat, the workers nursed their lunches under a grove of trees at the edge of the fields—as always, the men in one group, the women together in another.

"Just look at me!" Roxanne twirled, the hayseed dropping like confetti around her. "I feel like a cow."

"You're covered in the stuff." Rose frowned, pulling pieces of hay from her hair.

"Quit twirling like an idiot," hissed Prudence. "Don't you want the boys to think you're a grown-up?"

As she watched Peter join the men circling the barrels of water, Valerie tuned out her girlfriends' voices, which sounded to her like the noise of cackling hens. She took a long time wiping her hands on her skirt, careful to keep a distance from him. In line for a drink, Peter was bent over, examining something in his bag. He glanced up and caught her eye again. It froze her. Should she say something? She waited dumbly, watching the way his eyes flickered. Was it with recognition?

The harvesters in line behind Peter nudged him. He swung his bag over his shoulder and pushed his way past the rest of the hungry men, forgetting his food.

One of the girls tugged on Valerie's skirt, and she reluctantly sank to the grass, watching him go.

At the river's edge, a few villagers were swinging from a rope tied to an overhanging branch, daring one another into the cold water.

"Henry, go!" one of them called out.

Henry hurled his body off the edge of the embankment, holding tight to the rope and letting go at the highest point of the upward arc. Plunging into the water, he swam a few strokes and then emerged, teeth chattering. A dog ran up, barking its objection. Henry called to it. When it refused to come, Henry, feeling stiffened by the cold, rigidly tossed it a stick. The dog was distracted, though, by its owner bending to scoop up a drink of water. One of the visiting harvesters. More appeared lazily at his side—men exhausted by the day's hard labor, stooping, shuffling. But one approached the water to stand tall and dark in their midst.

Henry recognized him instantly. It was Peter.

Henry's heart pumped. Needing to think, he pulled in a huge breath and sank beneath the surface, making the world disappear. He opened his eyes to the calm of the green beneath. The current was not fast where he was, and he let himself hang, suspended by the water's buoyancy. He would stay there forever, in a peaceful world where there were no dead mothers. And no mother killers. *This is where I will stay*, Henry's submerged mind decided.

But his lungs decided differently, at first nagging, then demanding, and finally threatening to explode.

His head burst through the surface. His eyes blinked away the water. He looked to the shore—and blinked again to be sure.

The laborers were gone.

And Peter with them.

Some of the other boys had quieted, looking nervously at Henry. It was silent, except for a fluttering bird in the nearby pines. Henry's father seemed especially concerned. Adrien watched his son from the shore, but Henry refused to meet his gaze. Instead, he swam away furiously, in perfect form, his muscles burning, feeling as though they were going to tear open. The lesser shock of the cold was a comfort after the shock of seeing Peter.

He tried to swim away the horrible memory of the day Peter left town.

Even if he swam to the end of the world, though, it wouldn't be far enough to leave behind the image of his father, a tough man, tall and strong, bawling wet tears over his mother lying in the road.

Seeing Henry Lazar staring at him in horror had sickened Peter. Just like it had on that day so many years ago. He had to walk away before Henry emerged again from the water. He found an excuse—he told the men they should help set up the women's camp.

Why had he returned to the village? For so many years, Peter had avoided Daggorhorn, the site of the awful accident.

He hammered at a stake, driving it mercilessly into the earth, a rhythm to which he could sort his thoughts. There was something about Daggorhorn that had always called to him, he reminded himself. But he was afraid of being there. With *her*. His memory loved her too much. They had been just kids. Better to keep her as she'd been, hold her safe like a polished stone.

Coming in on the wagon, Peter had found his way as if

he were in a dream, pulled forward by an irresistible force to the village he had once known so well. How strange that everything in sight, every tree, every slight bend in the road, would remind him of the same girl, the one with the huge green eyes. And here she was, still.

Beautiful. A beauty so potent that it almost hurt.

But it prompted memories of a past he had tried to forget.

The horn sounded from the fields, signaling the end of lunch, signaling the end of memory. It was time to go back to work.

Why did I return?

The Reeve, the weary overseer, was pairing up the women, who would stomp the grass flat in the beds of the wagons, with the men, who would heave armfuls up to them. The Reeve's thick beard had gone wiry in the heat, like steel wool. Valerie stared ahead at the row of tightly knotted buns ahead of her and glanced to her left at the line of men, searching for him. Something drew her gaze to the middle of the line. Peter's liquid eyes were fixed on hers, and the distance between them seemed to radiate with a white heat. Valerie, without thinking, sidestepped a few eager women behind her and dropped back in the line. She would be paired with Peter.

The Reeve made his way down the aisle between the men and the women, tapping shoulders to assign partners. With his rough palm, he patted Valerie, then Peter, and he muttered "you and you" in a gruff voice. Though she heard the Reeve continue droning these same words down the line, she felt that, when said in reference to her and Peter, they rang out magically, making the connection between them tangible.

Her pulse was fast as they worked hard all afternoon, close together. She liked feeling the bales he'd only just held.

And yet, he never once looked at her. It was the *not* looking, though, that meant more than looking. Or was Valerie only imagining that?

The Reeve wove between the rows, constantly monitoring, and there was never a chance to talk. Eyes were on them all afternoon. It seemed she wasn't the only one who noticed the striking man — or remembered him. Every time Valerie started to lean down, set on saying something, someone else came by to cut her off.

The day slowly wound to a close, the sky turning a dusty gray-green. The Reeve stood nearby looking on, leaning on one leg, one ankle crossed over the other. His big, dark horse blinked its eyes slowly and watched, too, because there was not much else to see besides the villagers clustering together, hesitant to leave the day behind. The sooner the night came, they knew, the sooner the morning.

Having worked themselves too hard, they were useless now, their hands hanging limply by their sides, clenching outdated tools. They gathered in a mass like a swarm of locusts and laughed boldly as if they didn't have a care. Boys played tag, dodging one another, pulling at each other's shirts, their young bodies feeling awakened after the day's stiff work. They drank in the cool of the outdoors, feeling the way their roughened hands moved through the deadened evening air, hazy with hay.

Stacking her final bushel, Valerie saw Peter bending down for his sack, about to leave.

It was now or never.

"Peter..."

He straightened, his back to her like a wall. Then, slowly, he turned his face toward her and met her eyes. His gaze sliced through her like a knife.

Before she could stop herself, she asked, "Do you remember—?"

He took a step toward her. She felt the heat flare up between them.

"How could I forget?"

She felt weak with joy.

The supervisor blew his horn over the rusty, glistening crop fields, signaling the end of the day and the start of the campfire celebration.

Peter held her eyes a moment more before turning and walking away. Valerie watched from her perch in the wagon bed as he disappeared amidst the trees.

own by the river, a harvester was pulling fistfuls of feathers off a limp chicken, flicking them carelessly to the ground. Villagers were roasting another bird over a fire, rotating the long skewer. The ruddy smell of the freshly cut hay, rolled up into unruly bales, had awakened the villagers' animal instincts. They felt lustful in their exhaustion.

Valerie watched the men set out enormous kegs that, when empty, could be used for rides down the hill. Kegs like ones that Valerie and Peter themselves had spent some time in once, hiding from adults. The outer world had been reduced to a dull roar from the woody confines where they crouched, giggling.

Her memories of her time with Peter were smooth and compact, like eggs she could hold.

"How could I forget?" The new memory sliced through the old one.

Someone was playing a flute now, a haunting melody. Her father ate to the music, theatrically chomping down with every trill. "Helps the digestion," Cesaire said, motioning with his head to the flautist. It was the first time she'd seen him all day.

Valerie bit into the biggest chicken leg, her second. Prudence enviously measured Valerie's tiny waist with her two hands, her fingers touching. "It's not fair," she said.

Rose pulled the girls aside and led them down to the riverside to reveal an old rowboat that had been hidden in the shoreline brush that afternoon. It was faded gray from the sun, stained with bird droppings and traces of muddy water, the disappointing brown of coffee stains.

"This'll do," Valerie said with an approving nod.

Walking back from the river, Valerie saw that Peter had returned and that the Reeve had stopped in front of him. "We're clearing pines tomorrow and could use a man like you. We'll hire you on."

"You're a good worker," Cesaire added, unbidden. Valerie was surprised her father had spoken, but pleased.

Peter listened, looking doubtful.

"We'll provide you with an axe," the Reeve said. His cheeks were thick and roughened.

Peter whipped his own axe out from a back pocket, spinning it. "I've got my own. I want double, to chop trees."

The Reeve raised an eyebrow but reluctantly agreed to the price. The boy *was* a good worker. He had cleared more hay than anyone else.

"Okay." He turned. "Men on the big rocks other side of the river! The women will stay on this side." As per tradition, the men and the women would set up camp separately.

Despite the usual setup, Prudence's mother was concerned. It was the first year her daughter was there, and it was said that, long ago, someone had been killed there by the Wolf. Some said it had been a child; some said it had been three little girls who had wandered away during a swim. Others said it had been a woman who had run off after being caught with a lover.

As with so much of the Wolf lore, no one knew for sure exactly what had happened or to whom. Everyone knew only that something had happened to someone.

"I hope we'll be safe out here. Maybe my husband could stay." She always looked like she was about to sneeze or cry.

"Mother," Prudence said sternly, "it's nothing to worry about. The Wolf took a lamb last night from the altar. We're safe for another month."

"Women only," another woman said brusquely. "You'll be just fine."

"Okay then, girls." Prudence's mother pulled the girls close to give them private instruction. "Be sure to sleep with your shoes under your pillows. Don't want them getting stolen in the night."

The girls nodded in false solemnity. They were used to her eccentricities.

"But, wait, he hasn't sung yet. You'll want to hear it," one harvester called out, motioning to a squat man with a nose that sat on his face like a cucumber.

"Sing us a song, then. Get on with it," the Reeve ordered, no nonsense.

"I couldn't," said the squat harvester, falsely modest.

"Yes, you could."

"Oh, well, sure. I guess I could."

His song was winding and beautiful, a ballad. The villagers leaned back and let themselves be consumed by the sound, a sound that skimmed the river, that wrapped the woods, that brought everything together at once. Valerie closed her eyes but opened them again when she felt someone close to her. It was Peter. He had come very near, his breath warming her ear. "Find me later."

She boldly turned to look him in the face. "How?" Up close, he was jarringly beautiful. His thick, dark hair fell over one eye.

"Watch for my light."

All she could do was nod, stunned by her own physical reaction. She managed to collect herself, but he'd already gone.

After the men set off in boats to their campsite across the river, the girls gathered inside the tent they were sharing with Prudence's mother. Seated in a circle, weaving wreaths to serve as weights on top of the haystacks, they waited for sleep to overtake their fidgety chaperone. They had set up on smooth land and were circled around a large lantern, which had a design cut into it: Dots and squiggles radiated from the center, casting a world of shapes onto the ground and the tent's billowy canvas walls.

"The tea," Prudence whispered, holding out her open palm. Her mother was showing no sign of sleepiness. On the one night that they needed her to go to sleep, she was alert with worry, and Prudence wanted to make sure she didn't wake with every shifting of the fire logs. Valerie dug out a pouch of her grandmother's sleep-inducing sage tea from the depths of her satchel.

Prudence stepped outside the tent to prepare the sleeping brew, her eyes glinting as she bent over the fire's dying coals. She ducked back in and handed each girl a mug of plain tea, saving Grandmother's special brew for the last cup, which she handed to her mother.

They waited for her to drink it, trying not to look overinterested.

"Thank you." Prudence's mother raised it to her lips, then set it down.

"Too hot," she said, wincing.

The girls looked at one another. But soon, in her quick, nervous way, she picked it up again.

As she sipped her tea, the girls chatted about nothing, anything. The brew didn't seem to be having any effect. Within a few more moments, though, the girls looked down and she had curled up in her blankets.

"Now, girls, get to bed." That was all she managed to get out, propped up on her elbows, before feeling herself become weighty. Soon she'd fallen asleep and lay snoring on the ground. The girls pulled aside the tent flap, a window onto the pitch-dark men's camp across the river, anxious to see what the night would hold. Prudence coughed loudly, a test. Her mother did not stir. Now they could talk openly.

Roxanne couldn't contain her excitement. "Valerie, I saw *Henry* looking at you today."

"I don't know what to do," Valerie spilled out. "I think he was, too. I mean, he's nice. But that's...it."

"*Nice?* Valerie, he's *rich*!"

"I would kill to be in your position," Prudence said convincingly. "You shouldn't throw such an opportunity away."

"I just don't know," Valerie mused, thinking of the way she'd felt seeing Peter. "What is love supposed to feel like?"

"If you don't know what it feels like, then obviously you're not in it," Lucie snapped uncharacteristically. Valerie felt hurt. She did know, though, that while Lucie made

60

other people fall in love with her instantly, there was something that prevented her from being the girl whom every *boy* loved. Valerie knew it was a sensitive subject, and so, impressed with her own tact, she kept quiet.

"Can you believe Peter's back?" Roxanne asked, quickly changing the subject as she combed through her flame-colored hair with her fingers to dislodge any remaining straw.

"No," Valerie said, glad for the shift in topics, until she realized she couldn't be outspoken about this one, either. She shook her head to herself. "No, I really can't."

"He is so unbelievably gorgeous."

"I think he looks like a villain!" Lucie held an imaginary scythe and imitated his stalking gait, sending the girls into a fit. She closed her eyes when she laughed, something Valeire had always liked about her sister.

Prudence, though, remained serious. "Do you think he's killed people?"

"Like who?" Roxanne wondered.

"Like women."

Roxanne looked uncomfortable.

"What *I* can't believe is that you used to be his best friend," Prudence said to Valerie.

"They used to do everything together," Lucie said, a bit grudgingly. Valerie was surprised. Lucie did not seem like herself.

"Before he became a murderer," Prudence delighted in saying.

The girls considered this. Valerie had always been afraid to know the precise details of what had happened. It had been an accident. When Peter and his criminal father escaped town, their horse had reared up in fear, frightened by the mob and their torches—and Henry's mother had been struck. Valerie knew only vaguely of the incident, having been too young to be told at the time and the subject being unspoken of afterward—forbidden. Daggorhorn was like that. Traumas came and went. They had to be gotten over, and that was to be the end of it. But Valerie did know that Henry had never gotten over it.

"Wait," Prudence said. "I have something." She reached into her pack and pulled out a few jars. She had stolen some of the oak bark beer her father brewed in a large vat at the back of his herding shed.

"I figured he wouldn't notice a few jarfuls missing," she said.

The girls took turns downing small swigs of the burning liquid, but Rose was the most enthusiastic.

"I've heard it can blind you." Lucie scowled before reaching for a bottle.

Valerie tried it and spat it out. "Tastes like rotten porridge."

Prudence looked at her, offended. She didn't like it, either, but she felt somehow that Valerie's proclamation reflected badly on her father. "Fine, more for us, then," she snapped.

"Roxanne?" Rose offered the jar, teasing, already knowing the answer.

"I've heard that, too, about the blinding." She looked cornered. "Otherwise, I would," she added quickly.

"Suit yourself." Rose shrugged. Emboldened with drink, she blurted out what she'd obviously been dying to share. "Henry may have been looking at you, Valerie, but it was *my* shoulder he touched as he passed by in church this week."

"Touched how?" asked Roxanne.

"Very gently and sweetly." Rose demonstrated on Valerie. In one of her rare moments of girlish earnestness, she asked, "Do you think that's flirting?"

"I do!" Roxanne was optimistic.

Lucie flushed pink. She'd always been uncomfortable talking about boys.

"You're going to have to face them sometime, Lucie," Roxanne chided her. "Come on, you must think *someone's* handsome...."

Lucie beamed, and tears formed in her eyes from both laughter and embarrassment. Smiling, she leaned over and muffled her face in Valerie's lap.

The girls' conversation lulled as the night darkened to utter black. Together, they were comfortable without conversation, listening only to the elements of the outdoors.

Valerie gazed down at Lucie, who had fallen asleep in her lap, her hands clasped together under her cheek. Funny that sometimes it felt like *she* was the older sister.

"Do you ever wonder," Rose inquired, leaning into the circle, "what Henry looks like..."

"What he looks like?" Roxanne wrinkled her freckled snub nose, confused.

"Without his clothes on?" Rose blurted out.

"Eww! No! Do you?"

Rose smiled devilishly and tossed her hair. "I guess I do, if I'm asking." The scene Rose envisioned included, of course, a crackling fire, draped animal furs, and copious goblets of wine.

"I saw my father's once," Prudence cut in.

The girls squealed together, both thrilled and disgusted, then quickly quieted. Tea or no tea, they might wake Prudence's mother.

Lucie, cradled still in Valerie's lap, woke to their screams just as Valerie saw Peter's signal, a candle flickering dimly, on the other side of the river.

"Let's go!"

Lucie looked up at her foggily. "What's the rush?" she asked, narrowing her eyes. She knew her sister well. Too well.

"Because..." Valerie thought quickly. "We're wasting time. We need to cross the river now, before the tea wears off."

The girls looked at one another and then at the cool river lapping insistently at the shore. Valerie was right.

It was time.

As the rowboat slipped downstream, the paddling girls never suspected that Valerie was steering them in the direction of Peter's candlelight signal. The light had disappeared, but she had kept her eye on where it had flickered and knew just the spot in the darkness they should head to.

Roxanne leaned nervously over the side of the boat, eyeing her fractured reflection in the passing water. She felt the river looked like inky blood, but she tried to convince herself that it was closer to blackberry juice.

Prudence seized her opportunity. Hands on either side, she rocked the boat, sending Roxanne lurching back onto her seat, crying out.

Prudence laughed in a mean way, a savage playfulness lighting up her eyes.

Roxanne glared and splashed some water at her.

The girls could see three different campfires buried between the trees up from shore and began rowing competently toward them. These were girls who knew how to do things other girls didn't. They pulled at the oars, and the boat glided across the river like a solitary bird.

They considered briefly the possibility of getting caught but were able to put it out of their minds easily. They were young and free—and the risk seemed worth taking.

Seeing Peter's flashing light again, Valerie hooked the boat left. As it veered, Lucie lost her oar. Stretching out to recover it, she shifted her weight too quickly, causing the river to rush over the lip and into the boat.

The girls screamed as water came gushing in. Immediately they knew they had probably blown their cover.

"Jump in and flip the boat over! Hide underneath!" Valerie tried to shout and whisper at the same time.

The girls took in great surges of breaths and plunged into the water, pulling the boat upside down as they went. Reaching for each other underwater, they made their way under the boat. They rose up, skirts trailing behind them like shrouds, to meet in the air pocket underneath.

No one was happy. Their hair was dripping wet and their dresses soaked through, after all they'd done to be pretty for the boys.

They were here now, in the dirty blue underworld of a

rotting rowboat, kicking their legs furiously and yet utterly invisible to anyone watching, even to each other. All at once, it struck them as riotously funny, and together they convulsed with laughter, trying to hold it in. Then they buckled, letting their laughter spill out into the night in a few shrieks, but trying, too, to keep quiet. It sounded like they were inside a seashell.

Valerie was starting to enjoy her role as leader.

"We do need to deal with this," she said, stating the obvious. "And quietly," she shushed them. They strained to hear if there was any movement at the shore.

Roxanne nodded seriously to herself, as though Valerie had said something insightful. Prudence rolled her eyes, exasperated at Valerie's newfound tyranny.

After a moment of hearing nothing but the water swishing against the boat, Valerie decided they were still safe.

"Okay, here we go. One, two, three—lift!" Valerie said in a voice that was more commanding than it needed to be. The rowboat landed with one great plop, right side up. The girls waded through the shallow water onto shore, helping the boat along and feeling silly, the weight of their waterlogged skirts making their every step more slow and humiliating.

"Up here," came a loud whisper. Peering into the dark, the girls couldn't see who had spoken. They looked at one another, each privately trying to discern whether it could have been her own self-appointed boyfriend, before fastening the boat to a tree.

Valerie looked for Peter as they waddled up the river-bank. The fires danced up into the sky, and they moved to the one closest to them, feeling grubby, dirty around the edges. Lucie raced up first but veered away, whispering, "It's Rose's dad!"

"Hello? Who's down there?" came a voice from the circle of men crouched around the fire.

"Excuse us," Lucie said, putting on the voice of an old woman. The five girls tried to look huddled and shrunken, desperately repressing giggles.

The boys must be at the next fire.

As they neared its light, Valerie saw through the swirling sparks rising from the campsite that Peter was not among them. The harvesters who *were* there were happy to see the girls approaching but also seemed surprised.

"You girls came all the way over here?"

"Yeah!"

"How come?"

The girls looked at one another. *Didn't they know?*

"Um..."

Lucie jumped in. "Sorry. We always come over to this side when we camp out." It wasn't a lie. They'd never camped out before.

The boys looked at one another.

"We're not complaining."

The girls shrugged. The boys were not smart, but they were fun. They laughed when they saw how wet and bedraggled the girls were, but didn't laugh hard enough to

70

embarrass them. They were gentlemen, even, trying very hard to keep their eyes from straying to Rose's blouse, which had drooped even lower with the wetness, showing off her full figure. She did nothing to correct the situation.

As everyone dried off by the fire, Lucie set to work weaving crowns out of grass and clover, working deftly with her prunelike fingers.

"No flowers here," she quietly lamented to no one in particular. "These will have to do." She brightened as her work got under way.

Before long, one of the harvesters, Rose's or Prudence's, depending on which girl was asked, pulled out a fiddle. He wasn't a good player, but that didn't matter much. As the girls listened, the fire crackled, throwing up ashy bits that flew into their eyes.

Rose danced barefoot beside him, her skirt flouncing as she tried to rally the other girls to her side and her dark hair shining as it dried by the heat of the fire. Prudence and Roxanne held each other's hands and did a halfhearted circle step. It would have been easier, Rose thought, if they'd joined her in having more of the ale. Lucie came up and fitted the rings of clover onto each of their heads. She returned to her seat with one crown, displeased with the way she'd closed the loop.

"Was that you with the blinking light?" Rose asked the fiddler in a low voice that let him know he could confide in her.

But he didn't know what she was talking about. "Blinking light? Where?" He looked around, not wanting to have missed something.

Rose pouted. Guess not.

The group was too preoccupied to notice Valerie slip out of the firelight and into the darkness.

Feeling her way blindly through the dark field, her hands brushed the stalks of grass, dry and scratchy at the tips. When she ran her fingers along a blade the right way, from the bottom up, it felt smooth, but if she accidentally grazed a finger the other way, the blade struck back cruelly, like a thousand tiny knives.

She waited, scanning the void for Peter, but she saw nothing, heard nothing. She'd never minded being alone — often she preferred it, sought it out — but forlornly waiting for another person made her feel foolish and pathetic. Suddenly she hated herself and hated Peter. She started back toward the campfire, telling herself she'd never put herself in a position to feel so stupid again. It was then, as she trudged angrily through the reeds, that she saw the flickering glow of a candle in the forest. She took in a sharp breath, and her resolve vanished before her heart could pass another beat.

She stepped into the tangled dark of the forest, and it broke into motion. A few birds and insects were calling out in their separate registers, layering their songs, creating strange parallels and dissonances. She could smell the faint sweet odor of the woods at night, could hear the crinkling of dried leaves underfoot.

The candle, though, had disappeared.

"Peter?" Valerie called out in a whisper.

She stepped cautiously, wondering if she had only imagined his light, and if she really was as pathetic as she'd felt just moments ago.

But what was that on the ground? A marking? In the shape of...an arrow?

As she bent wearily down to rule out the possibility, just as she'd done so many countless times before, she felt a weighty, wet nudge at her back. A faint puff of air. Her breath snagged.

"Get on," she heard as she turned.

It was the damp, velvet nose of a horse. Peter was outlined against the night above her, loosely holding the reins.

A hand reached down for her, and she took it. It was coarse and calloused and warm. It gripped hers strongly, and without even thinking about it, Valerie let herself be lifted up, and she slid onto the horse, her body fitting into Peter's. She tentatively reached her arms around his waist and then tightened them when the horse moved. It was slow and careful as it stepped through the glade, Valerie's body dipping forward with Peter's as he moved to avoid low-hanging branches. They didn't speak. Valerie found that she didn't need to know who this new Peter was, that it was all right that she didn't, that in fact it was better not to.

And then Peter found what he'd been looking for—a path that cut through the forest. She held tight to him as he put their mount into a canter, and they rode, fast and free, through the woods. His body close to hers, Valerie recalled the electric thrill of being with him when they were young, running through the forest so fast that the air whistled in their ears. That feeling was still there, but it meant so much more now.

The horse picked up speed, the fast pounding of the hooves replacing the beat of her heart. The wind streaked through her hair, and she and Peter and the animal were so close and so powerful that it felt like they would just keep going forever together, flying.

But eventually, Peter turned the horse to circle back. Letting the horse walk, listening to its heavy breathing, they still hadn't broken the heavy silence. A man's voice suddenly shattered the quiet, shouting, "Hey! That's my horse! Get back here!"

Valerie hadn't registered that the horse wasn't Peter's. She smiled disbelievingly in the dark. Peter *was* dangerous.

"I'll wait here while you sneak the horse back."

"Don't go anywhere," he said, letting her off.

While she watched his dim outline ride off to return the horse, Valerie's chest felt squeezed, like there was too much inside, like something was trying to sprout roots and grow there.

Maybe that was what love felt like.

She tried to recall Peter's body, to feel him in his absence. He had smelled like tarnish and leather, this dangerous boy, this horse thief. She awaited his return, wondering what would come next.

Valerie heard a loud crackling of branches and looked around. Seeing nothing, she looked skyward, to the tangle of branches overhead. There were pockets of night visible between them, and she could see clouds becoming insubstantial in the sky and drifting into nothingness. Two clouds remained, though, and they drifted apart to frame the moon.

It took Valerie a moment to realize that the moon was full. And red.

Her mind was bleary with confusion. The full moon had taken place the night before, so how . . . ? Valerie's blood ran cold as understanding hit her. It was something the elders talked about, but not with much confidence. They quieted down whenever a question was asked, grumbling, as no one knew the answers with any certainty. They just knew it was not a good sign, like a black cat or a broken mirror.

Blood moon.

There was an unearthly growl in the distance.

Valerie sprang into motion, rushing out of the forest and down to the river's edge, which had been thrown into its own chaos, the swarm of people zigzagging to safety like bumblebees.

Everyone had scattered and was piling into boats, rowing toward the village. Valerie saw Roxanne and Rose rushing toward a boat just off the shore, sloshing through the water in a panic. A few harvesters had already climbed in—there was not much room left. Valerie hurried down to them, splashing into the water up to her waist.

"Girls, wait!"

"Get in!" Roxanne pulled at Valerie's hand, ushering her aboard.

"Wait! Where's Lucie?"

"She and Prudence went in the first boat," Roxanne replied, motioning urgently to a vessel already halfway across.

"Get in or don't!" one of the harvesters demanded as they pushed off. All niceties had vanished with the threat.

Once on the water, Valerie looked back to the shore, which was fading into darkness as the harvesters rowed furiously away. There was another boat waiting there and not nearly enough men to fill it. *Peter will find a place on it*, Valerie assured herself, an anxious sensation fermenting in her chest.

"The full moon was *last* night," a voice protested from one of the wagons everyone was piling into. The Reeve had them ready and waiting as the boats emptied. The wooden vessels creaked as they rushed inside the crumbling town wall. Men jumped out to slam the huge wooden gates of the village shut behind them.

"We should have been safe tonight."

"The blood moon has returned!"

As the wagon hurtled into the center of the village, everyone talked over one another in perplexed voices.

A few older men argued vehemently about how often they'd seen a moon like this one—twice or three times in their lives.

As the wagon made stops along the rows of houses, there were shouts: "Wolf night! Everybody inside!"

Valerie hopped off and dashed to her own cottage, hoping Suzette had slept through the commotion. But her mother was waiting for her up above, pulling her blue shawl tight against the cold. Her candle illuminated the porch, the uneven light falling upon Valerie.

Seeing her daughter, Suzette breathed a sigh of relief. "Oh, thank God." She let down the ladder.

"Mother?" Valerie wondered whether Suzette knew yet that she and Lucie had snuck off from the women's camp.

"Your father is out looking for you girls!"

"Sorry." The news didn't seem to have reached her.

"Where's Lucie?"

"She went with Prudence." Valerie was pleased with herself. It was true without implicating them in any wrongdoing.

Suzette peered down the road a final time but relaxed. "I'm sure your father will stop by there. Let's get you into bed."

Lying in their loft, Valerie's body missed Lucie's — it felt strange without her sister there beside her. She heard a rumbling of rain. It turned quickly to hail, which fell in solid stripes to the ground, too fast for the human eye to recognize single drops. Winter was coming, and the thunderstorm was cold, roaring like an angry God. Valerie wondered about Peter. There were flashes of light, after which the dark swallowed itself up again. Enveloped in storm clouds, the moon looked unclean, its red glow staining the sky.

That night, Valerie dreamed she was flying.

"I remember when I was a girl," Suzette was saying, seated on a low stool. "Eleven years old when I saw my first blood moon. I was young and crazy about a boy. It was almost romantic." Girlishly, she twirled a strand of her wavy, shoulder-length hair around her finger. "If it hadn't been so awful, of course."

Lost in her own thoughts, Valerie wasn't listening. In the morning, with chores to be done, last night's fears seemed trivial, the panic unwarranted. As she kneaded a mound of starchy, inelastic dough, her mind leapt from one thought to another. She wasn't worried about Peter, she decided, because he seemed like he knew things other people didn't.

She felt he could teach her his secrets and tell her about the world. She felt he could give shape to things, the way he used to carve saints out of shapeless wood blocks. But, she reminded herself, he was only there for the harvest...and her family would never allow her to be with him because of his history in the town.

Valerie pressed all her weight into the dough, irrationally annoyed with the difficulty of the task and the monotony of being indoors on a beautiful day. Yesterday had been the last day of fall, today the first of winter. She'd awoken this morning with the soles of her feet smooth and dry in the cold. She liked that. Now she heard voices outdoors but couldn't tell to whom they belonged until she heard the laughter. Rose's brazen laugh. She strained to hear whether Lucie was with her. Lucie was much better at baking than Valerie was, and ordinarily Lucie would have helped her after she finished her own. But she'd gotten off easy, staying the night at Prudence's.

"Anyway," Suzette concluded, realizing that Valerie wasn't listening, "I'd say we've got enough biscuits done now." She slapped her hands on the table decisively. "We'll... save your dough," she added, glancing at the unappealing brick Valerie was holding.

Valerie was withdrawn as Suzette wrapped the dozen hot barley biscuits and some cheese in soft white cloth and prepared to bring them to the men. Valerie could taste the dream she'd had the night before; it was fresh and sharp, like a lemon she had tasted once at a fair.

"Valerie, while I take lunch to the men, please clean up

here and sweep the floors. And then," her mother said, taking on a weary tone, "would you please fetch some water?"

"Yes," Valerie said, perhaps too quickly. "Yes, I'll go."

At the well, Valerie began to pull the rope, retrieving the pail from the water. She thought of the cool drink she was about to bring Peter, of how his eyes would peer over the cup as he drank, fixed on her. Imagining his penetrating stare, she stopped pulling, letting her body soften and her fingers ease off the rope. The pail plummeted and bashed violently against the stone wall of the well. She gasped and lunged for the rope as the pail splashed, breaking the surface of the water. Calmly and deliberately, she pulled up a new pail of water. Then she set off for the area where the men were clearing trees.

The dry scent of freshly cut wood stifled Valerie's nostrils as she approached.

The Reeve had assembled a group of well-trained men, and they were issuing heavy blows to the trees. He wasn't one to waste the chance to hire cheap laborers when they were in town. The men worked as a group, making the same motions, wearing the same clothes. But Peter stood out. He had slung his black shirt over his shoulder, revealing taut, tanned muscles. Resting herself against a tree, she watched his beautiful body torquing with each swing of the axe. It felt illicit seeing him in this way. But right somehow, too—she already felt he was hers.

Valerie was glad to see some remains of her mother's lunch discarded on the ground. Suzette had already come and gone.

"These acacias. They're too thick-skinned," Peter said to the Reeve, motioning to the thorny trees. He buried his axe in a nearby tree stump and left for a saw.

Valerie, seeing his axe unattended, darted forward to grab it and rushed back to hide behind a tree.

A nearby lumberjack had stopped his swing and balanced his axe on his shoulder. Leering down, he smiled at her and made a gesture of sealing his mouth shut.

She backed away. But she saw then that someone else had neglected his duties: It was Cesaire, sagging against a tree, bottle in hand, his eyes hollow. He was haphazardly raising spoonfuls of stew to his mouth, often missing the mark.

She looked away, as she always did. Her father was sloppy and helpless; he drank himself crippled. But he was also a woodsman, a hunter, strong and honest. It was hard to see him this way. Valerie felt conflicting emotions; he was a cause of both great pride and great shame for her.

Waiting, she began to wonder what was taking Peter so long to notice the stolen axe. But then he reappeared and immediately looked over to her hiding place. Her blood quickened. He was glad to see her, she could tell, but as he approached, he was somber, not giving her quite the warm welcome she'd expected.

Something was wrong. It couldn't be that he was angry at her for taking the axe—that wasn't like him.

He drew her farther into the cover of foliage so as not to be seen or overheard. She reached out to him. In the colder air, his hair felt so dry, thick, that she thought she could count the strands.

"Peter."

He shushed her, his finger grazing her lips. She misread his face and, for a moment, was annoyed; she didn't take well to submission. But she was too happy; the feeling melted away, and she forgot her anger.

"Why so sad?" She heard herself flirting, of all things. She couldn't help it; her heart felt like it was ready to flower.

"Give me the axe."

"What will you give me for it?" she replied.

He stepped toward her, but she backed up to a pine tree. He moved very close, but not touching. Seeing how serious he was, she surrendered, pressing the axe gently to his chest, letting her fingers spread out across the warmth she found there.

"Valerie..." Peter looked sad now. "They didn't tell you."

"What?" Valerie smiled. He was handsome when he worried. She wondered whether she was being annoying, or whether she'd be annoyed if she could watch herself as an outsider.

"Tell me what?" she asked impatiently.

"I heard your mother talking to your father earlier," Peter said, stalling. He fingered the torn shoulder of her light blue dress.

"And?" she asked quickly, reaching to pull at the tear in the fabric. She'd never worried much about her clothes.

"Valerie, Valerie." He saw that he'd have to tell her. He pressed closer. "You've been betrothed."

Her hand dropped from the unruly seam at her shoulder. She stared straight ahead at his sun-touched skin.

"To...Henry Lazar." It wasn't easy for him to say the name.

Valerie felt something fall to the floor of her stomach like a wet rag.

"No," she said, not wanting to believe him. "No, no," she told his chest.

Peter stood mute, wishing he could tell her what she wanted to hear.

"It's not possible," she said.

"It is. I'm telling you, it's done."

It's done. She tried to think.

"I mean...what if...I don't know if..." Valerie's thoughts were incoherent, but each time she spoke, it was with a note of urgency, as if she had hit upon a way to untangle herself from Henry.

"What do we do?" She leaned back against the tree.

Peter paced back and forth, rebelliousness shading his expression.

"Do you want to marry him?" Peter stopped in front of her, pressing close.

"You know I don't."

"Do I? Do we know each other anymore? It's been a long time. I'm not the same person I was."

"You are," she insisted. "I know who you are." She knew it was ridiculous, to feel so strong so fast...but she did. It just felt like they belonged together. She took his hand and held it tight.

His face softened. "All right, then. There may be one way...." he said out to the faint silver hue of the moors on the horizon.

Valerie looked at him blankly, her mind racing off on its own.

"We could run away," he said, speaking her mind before she'd quite reached the thought. He came even closer, almost touching his forehead to hers.

"Run away with me," he repeated the words, smiling a real smile, full and dark, in that terrifying way he had, as though his actions were self-contained, as though there were no consequences. She wanted to be a part of his ripple-less world.

"Where would we go?"

His lips brushed her ear. "Anywhere you want," he said. "The sea, the city, the mountains..."

Anywhere. With him.

He pulled back to look at her. "You're afraid."

"No, I'm not."

"You'd leave your home? Your family? Your whole life?"

"I-I think I would. Anything to be with you." She heard herself saying it and realized it was true.

"Anything?"

Valerie pretended to think a moment, for show, to be able to tell herself she had.

Then, almost meekly, "Yes."

"Yes?"

"Yes."

Peter let it sink in. They heard the chuff of a horse and then spied a hitched wagon in the distance, unattended, ready to go. No one was in sight. It seemed like fate.

"If we're going to do it, we need to go now," she said, thinking the same thought he was.

"We'd be half a day's ride away before anyone even knew we were gone," he agreed, giving her his rakish smile.

"Let's go then."

"I'll race you." He took her hand, pulling her through the glittering afternoon to the waiting horse. Water sloshed to the ground as Valerie abandoned her pail.

One day, she thought, *I will live with Peter in a home for us two, and there will be an orchard and also a narrow flowing stream where we will both bathe and swim. The sun will sing in the afternoons, and at night birds will tuck their heads under their wings in wait.*

The image became clearer the faster she ran.

Feeling the charge of freedom, she felt weightless, as though she were a dandelion seed being floated along in the air.

It was about that time when Claude found what he was not looking for.

Quiet Claude noticed things that no one else did. He noticed the way the tree branches flapped like wings, the way the grain waved like a storm at sea. He saw what was in the shadows and what was behind the shadows, too.

He took mystery seriously, and he tried to understand. What was not fathomable was why there was so much to see, so much beauty that he was forced to neglect with every moment. He had trouble focusing because he was focused on everything.

He carried a rawhide pouch into which he deposited those berries and petals whose pigments he found especially beautiful. He was a noticer and also a maker.

Today, he had constructed a tall scarecrow, clad in a floppy hat. The scarecrow was a skinny cross of bundled hay, its head bursting into a plume of wheat. Claude circled it, clapping, waiting for a response, an awakening into life. He was a magician, and he had faith in the magical.

Claude pulled out his deck of tarot cards, which he'd painted himself with materials he'd snuck from the kitchen:

dark vinegar and wine, beet juice, and stains from crushed carrots. He'd studied a deck brought to the town by a peddler. Despite the crude palette, the cards were colored with exact precision so that each character was vibrant and particular. He flicked a card from behind the scarecrow's head, a sleight-of-hand trick he'd been practicing. Gazing at it, he realized the dull morning light had brightened already into early afternoon. Startled by how long he'd been out, Claude began ambling toward home, sorting through the deck as he walked.

One orphan card, though, The Moon, escaped from the rest, flipping and spinning in the wind. Chasing it, scrunching his nose against the sun, Claude came upon an area of wheat that had been flattened.

It was stained with blood.

Claude could taste in the unsettled air that something evil had been there, and that he had arrived too late.

He followed the card hesitantly to something terrible, something that stopped him dead in his tracks. He stumbled to a halt.

What he saw was too awful.

Torn flesh, and the dirty hem of a yellow dress. The tarot card lay faceup near a still hand.

He hovered a moment, his body rigid with fear, and then he sprinted for the village, tripping over the knobs of obtrusive roots and ridges along the way. The scarecrow nodded behind him in the wind, seeing everything and nothing.

Running toward the wagon, Valerie felt impossibly free. She felt she was visible but unseen, like a blossom nestled into the brush that no one seems to notice.

The world was hers, and the beauty was everywhere. In Peter's tousled hair, in the rough wood under her hand as she vaulted into the seat, in the way the oiled leather reins caught the sunlight.

Dong.

Dong.

Dong.

The third toll of the church bells hovered in the air, and everything became still. Someone in the village had died. Valerie froze.

Dong.

A fourth toll shattered the silence. The world split open, exposing a raw inside.

Valerie and Peter looked at each other first in confusion, then in awful understanding.

The fourth bell meant only one thing: *Wolf attack.*

She had never heard the fourth bell, except for the time she and Peter had rung it themselves.

With those bells, Valerie knew.

Life would never be the same.

Part Two

8

Claude stood out of breath at the stairs to the boisterous tavern, knowing that he was not allowed to go in. Through the window, he saw huge pillars holding up candles the size of logs. He saw the tables, held together by wooden pegs, their surfaces scarred by decades of mug-pounding abuse. He could see, too, the light filtered through the hanging jars of wine, casting round red disks on the tables underneath. Deep red.

He saw it all, but he found he could not speak a word. He stepped just inside the doorway and waited.

Claude and Roxanne's mother, Marguerite, was working hard, carrying two trays on each arm, dodging rowdy drunks. She paused for only a moment as she passed her son.

"I'm working." She left him hovering at the door, looking repelled.

The noise of the tavern was deafening. Not knowing what else to do, afraid no one would listen, Claude yelled. Claude had the face of a much older man, deep creases stretching from his nostrils to the corners of his mouth. His skin was blemished, and people didn't like that, feeling it was the outward mark of an imperfect soul. And no one wanted to listen.

Marguerite came bustling out toward the noise.

"How dare you?" she asked cruelly, cutting through the silence.

Claude fell mute, breathing heavily, feeling a red flush break across his freckled face. Feeling sure he would not cause any more trouble, Marguerite turned to go inside.

But Claude yanked roughly at a fold of her dress.

"Cursed child," she muttered.

The tavern quieted, taken aback; he'd been too violent with her. Claude stood, paralyzed, shocked at his own actions, feeling exposed.

Someone snickered, though, tearing apart the quiet, prompting a raucous laughing fest. Behind their laughter, Claude knew, was fear. His own mother was suspicious of him and saw him as a foreigner. She did not understand where he had come from.

He wondered whether the Wolf would have been afraid of him in the way that the other villagers were.

Now both he and Marguerite were embarrassed. He shrank back to retreat.

The effort had exhausted him. He started to leave but burst back around. What he wanted to say was, "Lucie is lying in the wheat field mauled to death."

Stammering, though, all he *could* say was "W-w-wolf."

Finally, they listened.

It wasn't long before the bell began to sound.

The bell clanged louder, four tolls at a time, the closer Valerie got to the trail of villagers. She ran through the fields, dodging yesterday's haystacks.

"Don't believe the boy," someone was saying.

"Of course not. We all know very well that it's been twenty years and that the Wolf has never broken the peace," another called out over the clamor, bustling through the wrecked fields. "He probably just saw a wild dog and got confused."

Children were straining at their mothers' arms, hurrying them along. They wanted to see what all the upset was about. They were afraid they'd missed something, though they weren't sure what.

Valerie ran ahead of them, anticipating their destination. Reaching the center of the fields, she saw that some villagers were already there, divided into clumps. Seeing her, they quieted and held back, respectful. A woman could be heard at the back of the crowd sniffing up her tears. Valerie couldn't see past the clusters of mottled gray and brown cloaks, but she found Roxanne, Prudence, and Rose tangled in an embrace, each holding up the other two.

"Who is it?" Valerie demanded.

They turned toward her without breaking their knot.

No one could say it.

The crowd backed away so that Valerie could see her mother and father standing alone, their faces drawn in horror. She knew even before Roxanne whispered it.

"Your sister."

Valerie ran and fell before Lucie's lifeless body, clutching desperately at shreds of hay. She couldn't bring herself to touch her sister yet.

Lucie was in her finest dress, but the fabric was tattered and barely served to confine her body anymore. Her hair, a formal four-strand braid, plaited so carefully the night before, had loosened into matted strands.

The crown of weeds was still clinging to her hair. Valerie pulled off her own shawl and covered Lucie. Then she lifted her sister's hand to her cheek and felt a few shreds of paper in the cool palm, handing her one final secret. They looked like the remains of a note, but the writing was impossible to make out. Valerie shoved the pieces into her pocket.

The hand felt clammy with dew and gummy with clotting blood. She finally gave in to the exhilaration of grief, allowing it to bury her like a blanket of snow, so that everything seemed muffled and far away.

Soon Valerie felt anonymous hands intruding on her within the presence of her dead sister. She could not let go, because she didn't know whether her sister was gone from the body yet; she was not sure how fast the leaving happened. She had to be pried from the site, her knees stained dusty brown with blood and winter soil, tears streaming down her cheeks.

As she was dragged away, the first snow of the season began to fall.

Winter was early.

Within an hour, the cottage was so full of villagers that there was no air left to breathe. Valerie felt scooped out like an empty gourd.

The family was grieving separately, stunned. It felt as
though the entire world were different, even though their
surroundings were, impossibly, the same. Aside from one
of them being gone, everything else was as it had always
been. A string stretched across the room, drooping under
the weight of the family's laundry. The biscuits were drying on the rack. Everything was as they'd left it.

Suzette had taken up a position by the door, watching
the outside because she couldn't bear what was inside. The
sparkle of snow just coming down made it look like glass.
Valerie wondered if her mother was disappointed with what

she had left, now that the more beautiful, the more loving, the more obedient of her daughters was gone.

Across the room, Cesaire tossed back his head, going for a sip of his flask. He was tormented and stoic, refusing comfort even from Suzette. Valerie wished he could be less hard on himself. It seemed as if he felt responsible for Lucie's death, for not protecting his daughter.

Mourners milled about, aimless, in shock. They were bland in their sympathy, saying those empty things that all people say to grieving families.

"She's in a better place now."

"Good thing you have Valerie."

"You could always have another...."

Claude and the girls were dressing Lucie's body, washing it tenderly, her face, her hands, but they felt sick lifting her too-heavy limbs. Swaddling Lucie, feeling her body, making it beautiful with flowers, seemed obscene.

Valerie stood beside them but did not move or speak. Her friends wanted to support her but didn't know how. Almost afraid of the rigid intensity of her grief, they left her alone.

Villagers felt they should be speaking of Lucie, but what to say? They were thinking of her, and perhaps that was enough. They sat in corners, conversing in guilty whispers, unable to focus wholly on grieving, as they were fretful about the coming night. The blood moon would rise for a second time tonight, that much the elders were able to agree on. Men looked at their own daughters and wondered who might be next.

"W-w-why does the Wolf hate us?" Claude finally asked, and for once people quieted as he spoke.

A simple question. And yet no one could answer.

Roxanne coughed, the polite little noise filling the room.

A knock at the door dispelled the tension.

"It's the Lazars!" Valerie vaguely heard her mother say. All the other girls looked up as the three generations of the family entered — Madame Lazar; her son, Adrien, the widower; and his son, Henry. Rose offered a thin-lipped smile at the youngest, but Henry searched only for Valerie. When her eyes didn't even flicker in his direction, when she shrank back from him, he bowed respectfully and didn't try to approach her.

He knew that Valerie kept things to herself.

Sensing Henry there, and her mother's displeasure with how she'd treated him, Valerie wanted to resent him but found she didn't. She knew, though, that mixed up in his affection for her was the problem of pity. She looked to her father, who nodded, before she retreated up into the loft bed she had shared with Lucie.

She gently touched the cornflowers Lucie, a lover of beauty, had hung to decorate her side of the bed. The grief made Valerie feel like her skin was stretched too thin. Like she couldn't get enough breath in, as if her lungs had grown shallow.

Madame Lazar lifted a hand to pat her gray hair as she

assessed the cottage with a mask of disapproval. She was an old woman who had forgotten how to be around groups of people—which was all right, because her fixed gaze made most uncomfortable. They did not like, either, the way she smelled. Like starch and garlic.

"I am so sorry for your loss," she said to a broken and stunned Suzette.

Adrien followed, moving to shake Cesaire's hand. Adrien was still ruggedly handsome, his face slightly lined in that masculine way.

"Lucie was a good girl," he said.

The past tense came as a shock. Cesaire was not ready for it. He had a habit of swishing his drink around in his mouth when he didn't like something. Suzette shook her head from across the room, and Cesaire knew what it meant: Put down his cup.

Claude, either wanting to include her or else feeling mischievous, performed his disappearing and reappearing tarot card trick behind Madame Lazar's ear. She fanned him away.

Out flicked a card.

Trying a different tactic, she held her teacup high and tried to pretend he didn't exist.

Turning from the scene below into her bed, Valerie smelled Lucie, the scent of oats, of warm milk, of someone she could trust. She knew the scent would fade, that she would lose even that. Valerie pulled aside a knot of wood to reveal a secret hiding place dug into the ceiling and removed a sprig of velvet-wrapped lavender.

Valerie remembered when her mother used to take her and Lucie for long walks. They would pass the grain field, where the thin stalks swayed with the easy rhythm of the wind. The three of them would then reach a clearing that was bright with lavender. The girls would gather the flowers, Lucie carrying them in her skirt, until their fingers were raw and they had to go crying to their mother, and Suzette would always have remembered to bring the salve.

Removed from the scene, Valerie looked down again at the main room of the house. She felt comfortable in her usual position as watcher, up above, separate. Voices moved with fluidity in and out of focus. Faces came and went. She stared through people, finding it hard to believe they were real. The villagers talked over one another, but no one was saying anything. Valerie sank into the drone, letting the tide of voices wash over her.

Her sister's body below lay still, like a piece of furniture. All the people put in the obligatory visit, hovering around it, feeling they ought to look at the body but feeling like voyeurs when they did, then trying to move away before too long.

Suzette was seated on a low stool near the fire. Valerie saw her looking for a long time at Henry. Her mother was nervous around him; it almost seemed she wanted him more for herself than for Valerie.

Valerie lay down on her side, and sleep swept her up like a wave, held her in its buoyancy, and carried her.

She woke up, remembering a time long ago when Lucie had been walking home around dusk. Valerie had pretended to be the Wolf, sneaking up behind her, snarling and then pouncing. What to their parents was a matter of life and death had been just a game to two little girls. Although she comforted her weeping sister, Valerie had realized then that there was something destructive, even predatory, inside herself. After witnessing Flora's sacrifice, though, she never scared her sister again.

She tortured herself with this memory awhile, opening the wound the way she would pinch her skin together after a scrape to make the blood come more quickly. Valerie peered out over the edge of her loft. The Lazars still lingered and her friends dozed on stools, their red, black, and brown hair bobbing in sleep. She saw her mother seated at the table alone, looking up meekly, bathed in the eerie light of a single candle. Seeing her daughter awake, Suzette moved to the loft.

"There is good news in the midst of this difficult time, Valerie," she said, ascending the ladder to bring herself to Valerie's level.

"I have already been told that I am to marry Henry Lazar. Just tell me whether it's true," Valerie whispered back.

Startled, Suzette recovered her composure.

"Yes, Valerie," she said in a put-on voice, rolling her wedding ring between her thumb and first two fingers, with a veneer of joy. "Yes, it is true."

Valerie felt the life being torn out of her. In this grief-filled moment she realized how strong her feelings were for Peter, whom she had lost in the commotion of the day. She longed for him but felt guilty for thinking that way under the circumstances.

"Mother, it feels wrong to talk of this now."

"You're right," Suzette admitted sadly. "Now is not the time. There will be time for all this later."

She stroked Valerie's hair. The sound of Suzette's voice was somehow both nerve-racking and comforting. "But it's true that Henry is your fiancé now," she added. "You should let him offer his condolences."

Valerie looked at Henry down below, seeing the concern marking his kind, handsome face. "I barely even know him."

"You'll learn to. That's what marriage is."

Valerie would not, she could not. "Not now, Mother."

Suzette made the decision to try a little harder. "You should know something....I didn't love your father when we were married. I was in love with someone else."

Valerie stared at her mother, in all her complexity.

"His mother wouldn't allow us to be together. But I grew to love your father, instead. And he gave me two beautiful daughters. Now go down there. Please."

"I said no," Valerie snapped, swallowing her unasked questions.

Suzette knew this side of her daughter's character and knew better than to fight it. She slunk back down the ladder, plastering on a composed face, as Valerie had never been able to do.

Henry, meanwhile, had witnessed the tense scene. He turned to Cesaire.

"Come with us to the tavern." He put a steadying hand on the older man's shoulder. "We will let the women grieve in their own way," he said with his characteristic grace.

Cesaire nodded, glad to leave.

Adrien, too, looked grateful for an escape from the overbearing atmosphere of the cottage. Kind as he may be, he had never been a man who was particularly open with his emotions. Valerie knew that he had always been good to Lucie and that her death must have brought up memories of his wife's passing. It could not be easy for him.

Henry gave the sleeping loft a gentle nod as he shook on his long leather coat before following his father out of the cottage.

"I can't believe she's gone."

Valerie finally descended the ladder to where Lucie's body lay. She had no tears left, only a vast emptiness.

Suzette packed up the food that had been brought, each dish nudged at by a knife or two; no one was hungry now. The other girls still sat around Valerie but didn't say much. Needing something, anything, to do with themselves, they touched whatever was around. It kept them from feeling useless.

Roxanne sadly fingered Lucie's long woolen dresses. Prudence secretly coveted Lucie's sheepskin cloak and petted its fleece possessively, hoping someone might suddenly offer it to her.

"How is it that nobody saw anything last night?" Madame Lazar blinked, breaking the silence. She turned to Valerie. "Weren't you with her?"

Valerie began tying ribbons into her sister's hair and gave no answer. She thought of the pieces of paper she'd found in Lucie's grasp, but the pieces didn't fit together and the dew had dissolved whatever message had once been written there. It must have been a note, but what did it say? Was it an invitation out to the fields? From whom?

Her world was reeling around her, and she couldn't focus on Madame Lazar's face—everyone was passing in front of her like wagon wheels spinning by.

"The beast lured her away." A distraught Suzette jumped in, uncomfortable with the subject.

"She was with you." Roxanne turned to Prudence. "I know I saw her in your boat."

"She *was* in my boat, and then she said she was meeting you."

"I just don't understand why she would say that. It isn't true." Roxanne shook her head.

"Maybe she went to meet a boy," Prudence suggested in a snaky voice.

"My daughter had no interest in boys," Suzette said quickly.

"She was very taken with my grandson," Madame Lazar announced. She had a way of speaking so that her words crept into the mind as though they had been there all along. "She used to come by and follow him around like a puppy. If she had just found out that Henry was engaged to her sister..."

The girls froze and then looked at each other to see if anyone had known this huge secret. Valerie looked down at her lap and shook her head. She wished she could have told her friends herself. She knew they all dreamed of themselves on Henry's arm.

Rose huffed for a moment but shrugged it off, thinking, *Henry's eyes could still wander.* Prudence glowered but knew she couldn't say anything here. Roxanne turned her thoughts back to Lucie—she knew Henry had never been meant for her.

"It must have broken Lucie's heart," Roxanne finally said in a rapt whisper.

"Maybe she *chose* to die rather than live without Henry," Rose added dreamily. "She went out seeking the Wolf."

"No," Suzette amended sternly. "It's unthinkable."

"She never told me how she felt," Valerie thought aloud, feeling the betrayal in her gut. How had she been so blind? Her sister had loved Henry silently. *Did she know about the engagement? Did she overhear our parents planning?* Valerie supposed it was possible, but it seemed unlikely since they were always together. *Would it have broken her heart?*

"Don't worry, you poor child," Madame Lazar said, seeming almost disinterested in the subject of Lucie's death. "I know you're worried about your sister, but Henry always had his eye on you. You are—were always the pretty one." She reached out to stroke Valerie's cheek, moving like a spider.

Suzette was thinking she'd rather the visitors begin to leave, but hearing steps ascending the ladder, she still opened the door, moving onto the porch in anticipation and closing the door behind her against the snow. But when she saw the dark head of hair come into view, she wished she hadn't. She recognized him even after all these years.

"For Lucie," Peter said quietly, the flame of a gilded saint's candle fluttering in his hand.

"Leave."

Peter had anticipated this reaction and was prepared. He

cleared his throat. "I'm paying my respects," he said, still trying to be polite. The woman was grieving for her daughter.

"I can guess the reason you're here. I've just lost one daughter," she said, her hand on the door. "I won't lose another."

"Wait."

"She's all I have left," she said. "And you have nothing to offer her."

Peter knew that she was right, that Valerie deserved better. But he could not give her up.

"I have a trade. The same trade as your husband."

"I know exactly what a woodcutter earns."

Peter began to protest, but Suzette stopped him. "Henry Lazar is her only hope for a better life."

Peter looked into Suzette's anguished eyes, her words hitting him somewhere deep. It sank in: He could not give Valerie a good life.

"If you really love her," Suzette said, her voice cracking, "you'll leave her alone."

They stared at each other, eyes sparking with conflicting emotions. Peter broke first, backing away, angry at her dismissal and at himself for understanding.

She went inside and shut the door, resting her back against it. She would tell the room that it had just been a laborer paying his respects.

Climbing back down the ladder, Peter realized that,

filtered through and behind the agony, there was something about the letting go that felt good.

He was someone who had a conviction, who believed in the value of something and held it as sacred.

It was just that nothing had ever held such value for him before.

10

Peter walked through the quiet town, hushed by the
snowfall, grief hanging in its very air. The men
were in the tavern, the women still home mourning. The town was unified, even beautiful, in its broad
stillness.

Stepping through the tavern's back door, he saw that a
full candelabrum was dripping wax into the same corner it
had dripped into for years, collecting into a towering castle
on the ground. No one bothered to clean it up, least of all
Marguerite, who had enough on her hands as it was.

Seeing the barrel kegs banded with rusted metal, he recalled
a long afternoon once spent in the body of an empty keg
with Valerie. He wondered whether she remembered.

As he slid along the back wall, Peter heard Father Auguste

say, "I've summoned help." The local priest was tall and anxious. Like a daisy stem, he was upright and purposeful, but still fragile and thin.

The Reeve eyed the priest and waited to hear more. He bit into an onion he'd been peeling.

"From someone closer to God," the holy man went on. Father Auguste wore on a chain a simple ampule that held holy water and protected him from evil. He held it in his hand now, as if it would bring him closer to his idol. "Father Solomon."

The room quieted. *Father Solomon*. He was legendary, a priest and a renowned werewolf hunter who had destroyed beasts throughout the kingdom. He was resourceful, brave, and cunning and would stop at nothing to eradicate evil. It was said by itinerant merchants that he traveled with a small army, warriors hailing from Spain, North Africa, the Far East.

"Who gave you the authority to do that?" The Reeve stepped in front of him.

"God. The highest authority."

"You can plan for the next life," the Reeve growled, rolling up his sleeves. "I will plan for this one."

"But the Lord—"

Adrien pushed his chair back and stood up.

"This is a village matter," he said decisively. "We will kill it ourselves."

The Reeve chewed on his onion, nodding.

Cesaire breathed in a slight whistle, as if cooling the

116

roof of his mouth after sipping something that was too hot. The villagers turned to him. It had been his daughter killed. He nodded his approbation of Adrien's words.

"Father Solomon would rob us of our vengeance," Cesaire said.

"She was your child, but—" Father Auguste looked at Cesaire pleadingly.

"We are here," Adrien persisted, "to right a wrong. Today, we must stand united to say that we will fight not only to avenge our past but also to *renew our future*. To show the beast that we refuse to live in fear." He strode behind the empty bar and rested his weight against the counter.

"Maybe Father Auguste is right," Henry started thoughtfully, rising from a bench. "Maybe we should wait."

From the back of the tavern, Peter stifled a burst of laughter. Henry gripped the edge of the table.

Adrien turned to Henry with a withering glare.

"Maybe, my son," Adrien said quietly, "you should find your courage."

Henry took a labored breath.

"You want to hunt the Wolf?" He narrowed his eyes, spurned. "All right, then. Let's hunt it."

The Reeve, wide and stout with hands the size of iron pots, pounded his mug on the table aggressively.

"We've let this go on too long. We are here to win back our freedom!" he cried, rallying the men. He pulled the silver dagger from his pants waist and stabbed it into the table.

The men shook their fists in the air in approval.

117

"Let's kill that *goddamn* Wolf!" he shouted.

"I'll drink to that," Cesaire said, downing what remained in his cup. It was early evening now, and the group realized they'd better get on with it. They began to file out the door to prepare for the hunt.

Father Auguste teetered. "Wait! We should *wait* for Father Solomon!"

But his hysterical voice was lost in the chorus of deep voices and clanking mugs.

Cesaire stopped to refill his cup, and, on the way out, he dumped the whole of it on Father Auguste's head, putting a stop to his protestations.

The men rushed out of the tavern into the gray light. They were rowdy while crunching through the new snow, throwing their hats into the air and swinging their jackets over their heads. They felt bigger than themselves, swelled with purpose.

Their wives heard the clamor and chased after them, running back for packs of food and warm scarves. The snowfall was getting heavier, bringing true winter earlier than usual.

It will be me, each man thought. *I'll be the one to do it.* They barely saw their women or their children, and made a point not to notice their troubled faces.

Drawn outside by the noise, Valerie looked around for

Peter. She was angry that he hadn't come by the cottage to comfort her, but she wouldn't let him leave without saying good-bye.

She found him in the crowd right away, his dark hair and black cloak standing out against the white snow. Her mother's words rang in her head. She wondered if it would be wrong for her to marry for love when her mother had not, for her to experience a greater love than her mother ever had.

Seeing her, Peter sidestepped into a shed. It was hard to tell whether his face had darkened when he'd seen her, or whether it had only been the dimming light. Pushing her thoughts aside, Valerie climbed down and followed him into the cobwebbed dustiness.

"Be careful," she said, reaching her fingers to his. "I just lost my sister. I can't lose you, too."

She felt him pull back. Her hand hovered in the air and then dropped, fingertips tingling with want.

Peter looked at her, also aching to touch her but trying to be strong.

"I know. But, Valerie, this is all wrong."

"What is?"

"We can't do this."

Valerie didn't understand. All she saw was Peter's tortured face. *I will save him*, she thought.

"You have to go through with it. You have to marry Henry," he said.

Confused, she shook her head like she had tasted something bitter.

"But I want to be with *you*." She felt like an idiot saying it, but she meant what she had said—she could not lose him, too.

"Your sister just died...."

"No. No, how dare you use that!" Peter hadn't even bothered to pay his respects. And now he was trying to lay claim to Lucie's death.

"Valerie. Don't make this something that it's not," he said, hardening himself to her. "It was what it was. Nothing more." He said it smoothly, with precision.

Valerie stepped back with the sting of the words.

"You don't believe that," she persisted, shaking her head.

He was unflinching, though, his face uncompromisingly austere. He refused to look at her. But he touched a strand of her long blond hair with one finger. He couldn't help himself.

Feeling an angry wrench in her throat, she pushed him away roughly and burst back out into the crowd. She walked toward her cottage, but her body felt dead inside her clothes.

"Valerie, I've been looking for you."

It was Henry Lazar. She met his brown eyes reluctantly, seeing the contrast between him and Peter. Henry's eyes were open, giving, hiding nothing... or perhaps there was just nothing behind them.

Valerie glanced back and saw no sign of Peter. She tried to collect her shattered feelings.

"I made something. For you."

Henry could tell that her mind was elsewhere, but he forged on.

"I'm sorry, I know this is the wrong time. What you're going through...I should have waited...." He glanced over her shoulder and saw Peter melting into the crowd. "But in case I don't return, I wanted you to have this."

Valerie was set against loving Henry, against even liking him. His charm, his sweet uprightness, could never sway her now.

But he reached inside his pocket and retrieved a thin copper bracelet. It was simple and elegant, hammered into tiny pecks and delicate ridges.

"My father taught me to make this, to perfect it, to one day give to the woman I love."

In spite of herself, Valerie was moved. It was something given in the midst of everything taken.

"You will be happy again," he said with a slightly knowing air, clasping the bracelet around her wrist. "I promise." Valerie felt oddly consoled.

Adrien approached, put a hand on Henry's shoulder, and beckoned him into the rowdy pack of men marching out of the village. Henry squeezed her hand and then squared his shoulders to join the crowd.

Valerie stood with the other women, watching the men go. She couldn't help bristling at this division of the sexes. Her fingers itched to hold a weapon, too, to *do* something, to *kill* something with her anger.

She spotted her father trudging soundlessly at the back, wrecked within the depths of his heavy coat. She hurried to him. His eyes were broken, like something shattered.

"I'm going with you," she told him, trying to keep the pity from her voice.

"No."

"But she was my sister."

"No, Valerie." He slung his axe over his shoulder. "This is not for women."

"You *know* I'm braver than most of those men. I can—"

Her words were cut off in surprise as she felt his hand grip her arm. She hadn't felt his strength since she was a little girl gazing up at him in his supreme fatherly heights.

"I will take care of it," he said, his eyes wild. "You can't go. You're all I have left. Understand?"

In that moment, she saw her father and she admired him again. He was returned, in all his strength. And it felt good and right and safe.

She nodded.

"Good."

He loosened his grip.

Then, like watching a candle die out, she saw the fatherly strength leave him, and the sad man who was left behind shrugged his shoulders and smiled his smile that for years had been saying, *Yes, the joke's on me, but at least I know it.*

"If I never return, you, my daughter, are the heir to my bedpan," he joked.

She couldn't laugh. She watched him disappear into the group.

He can't even swing his axe to meet a chink in a tree, she thought. *How will he confront a ravening beast?*

Valerie turned back to the cottage, thinking of the sage brew she had left in her satchel.

When all the women had trickled back into their houses and her mother was in the throes of sleep, thanks to a dose of Grandmother's tea, Valerie did what she had to do. She tossed on her nubby gray cloak with the frayed bottom and scrappy leather collar.

She knew where they were headed, where the Wolf made its lair. She had seen bones on the trail to Mount Grimmoor and in the Black Raven Woods. Following the last of the men through the lonely village, she sidestepped into the lightless alleys to avoid being seen.

She listened and watched as she took a parallel path — seeing what men do when they're alone together like a pack of wild animals.

Claude, bearing a pitchfork and a kitchen knife, appeared in the makeshift war garb he had assembled out of old pots and pans.

"I-I-I'm coming," he said earnestly. As he spoke, his hands darted out to either side like flighty birds.

"No beasts allowed," one of the men called out. The

group laughed, nudging Claude away. Valerie wished she could go to him and was glad when she saw Roxanne come hurrying after to usher him home. Valerie felt sorry for Claude but agreed he should be kept safe at home.

She saw Cesaire catch up with Adrien at the front of the crowd. He looked imposing and angry, his boots scuffing along the snowy ground as he moved bravely forward.

"Fancy a nip?" Some spirits sloshed out of the uncapped mouth as he offered his flask.

Adrien held up a hand in refusal. Cesaire shrugged and took a long drink.

"Thank you for standing up for my Lucie," Cesaire said.

"We'll be family soon." Adrien nodded. "You would have done the same."

Valerie had never seen the two of them so companionable. Who would believe that the richest man in town and the town drunk could find common ground? She supposed even a drunk might have something a rich man wanted: a piece of property to add to the family treasure. Valerie's cheeks flushed as awareness set in—*I am only a thing to be traded*.

Valerie's eyes darted after a white rabbit, barely visible against the snow. She caught the flash of a pair of wet black eyes. Now, though, was no time for distractions.

She saw that Peter and Henry were treading sullenly along either edge of the path in a dead heat, neither willing to fall behind the other.

They were wary, curious about each other, but each dared to look only when he was sure the other's eyes were averted.

Moving quickly to keep up and stepping lightly to avoid sound, Valerie glanced up at the bulging crimson moon, pregnant with warning in the night sky.

She could not bear to lose anyone else tonight.

11

Sensing the black rush of crows lifting into flight from the shimmering white forest floor, Grandmother knew the men were coming. She stepped onto the porch to wait.

And soon they were there. The men looked up at her as if she were a fearsome goddess, the flames of their torches rippling the air as they either moved past or stood by, waiting to catch a glimpse of Grandmother. She was a legendary being, outside of time. She was beautiful and young for her years, though she'd aged some today with grief. Her hair was wound into dreads by gray cord, her tear-stained cheeks showing no wrinkles. It was no wonder people accused her of witchcraft. She climbed down, carrying a candle to illuminate the steps.

"Son," she said to Cesaire, embracing him, "I heard about our Lucie." She didn't explain how. "Promise me you'll be careful, my boy." She handed him the pack she'd assembled.

"Don't worry. The Wolf has no interest in me," he said, smiling through his pain. "I'm all gristle."

Grandmother ascended the stairs, her heart heavy. From her porch she was watching the group move on when one of the men, the last in the line, veered off and began to climb up after her. Grandmother could feel the creak of the wood as the figure set its weight on each step. He moved quickly: up, up, up. Grandmother shuddered as the uninvited visitor rose onto the deck.

Stalking up to her, the figure flung back the hood of his cloak and—

It was Valerie.

Grandmother shook her head, her tension uncoiling into laughter. "Sweetheart, darling, what are you doing?"

Valerie frowned. "Why shouldn't I go with them? She was my sister."

Grandmother sighed and took her in her arms. "You're frozen already in this thin little cloak. I don't think you'll make it."

"Well, no, I guess not," Valerie said, shivering as Grandmother led her inside with a jangle of her charms and amulets.

It heartened Valerie to be there, in Grandmother's wild

128

tree home. Branches grew through the roof, and winter dandelions popped up through the floorboards, and there was some sort of nest in every nook. The tree house was packed with curious things. Valerie let her eyes roam through the small interior. Mollusk shells like giant ears, a pincushion inlaid with mother of pearl, a horn cup, dried yams, a vulture's talon. The frayed hems of dusty peacock tapestries in faded pinks and blues brushed against endless rows of bottles topped haphazardly with cockeyed corks. An enormous kettle of tea quivered on the stove.

Valerie loved Grandmother's way of life, even if it was the topic of local lore and ridiculed by the villagers. Even if the price Grandmother paid was that some blamed her for the Wolf's presence in the village.

"You'll need your sleep." Grandmother handed Valerie a steaming cup of her sage brew.

Valerie neglected her tea and stood at the window, watching the men make their way through the dark forest. She faced the crag and saw the cold wind pushing through the trees, wet with snow, and heaving gustily like a young child blowing out birthday candles. The wind tugged at the men's torches as the last of them jogged up the steep rock and disappeared into the cave. One torch belonged to her father, one to the man she loved, and another to the man she might have. All were reduced to points of light glinting in the distance. Feeling her stomach coil, Valerie stepped away from the window.

Who will come back? Will any of them? Another sudden gust of wind unnerved her. Frightened, she felt the ease with which it shuddered the foundation of the tree house, the thick trunk, and its heavy branches.

Nothing was right.

Lucie was gone.

Valerie could feel it, the absence of beauty. She knew Lucie was beyond the bounds of their loft, of the village, of the land and the world. That she was now in an else-place, a non-place.

"I'm her sister. I should have been with her," Valerie blurted out, sinking into the couch.

"You can't blame yourself," Grandmother said, setting down a bowl of stew. Grandmother stooped to sprinkle some crushed bitter herbs over the bowl. They tasted like something that wasn't supposed to be eaten.

"Of course, as my own grandmother used to say, 'All sorrows are—'"

"'—less with bread.'" Valerie filled in her half of the line she knew so well.

Grandmother tried to smile weakly. Valerie didn't bother.

"Are you still cold?"

Valerie realized that she was.

Wordlessly, Grandmother left the room. Valerie watched as the snow-laden limbs swayed in figure eights in the sweeping wind. Grandmother came up behind Valerie and draped something over her shoulders.

"How's this?"

Valerie looked down. It was a beautiful, bright red cloak.

"Grandmother..." Valerie had never seen anything like it. It was the red of far away, of fantasies, an overseas red, a red that Daggorhorn had never seen, a red that did not belong there.

"I made it for your wedding."

Valerie looked down at her bracelet.

"The wedding doesn't feel like mine. It feels like I'm being sold." Peter's words clutched at her, but she said nothing about them. She knew that her parents did not approve of Peter, but what if he avenged Lucie's death, if he came back having slain the Wolf? She began to fantasize about his redemption. But then the sting of Peter's words came flooding back, and she knew that none of that mattered now.

"There's someone else, isn't there?" Grandmother leaned forward.

"There was someone..." Valerie said slowly. "But maybe there isn't now."

Grandmother nodded. She seemed to be able to make sense of Valerie's nonsensical explanation.

"I just can't believe he'd give me up so easily."

Grandmother sipped her tea. "Maybe there's more to the story." Valerie shook her head, trying to dismiss the thoughts.

"Maybe. I hate to think of it now, in the wake of Lucie's death."

"How I wish you could follow your heart," the older woman said finally.

Valerie thought she saw a flash of anger cross her grandmother's eyes.

"There's little chance of that." Valerie's own face darkened in reply. "All my mother cares about is money, and my father's too drunk to notice half of anything."

Grandmother turned, a smile playing on her lips. "You, Valerie, were never one to mince words."

Valerie and Grandmother soaked in the silence, letting what had been said with such lightness weigh heavy upon them. The bells Grandmother kept out front tinkled in the wind.

"When I was young," Grandmother began, her voice soothing the tense air, "the Wolf would attack entire families. Lure them out into the wild."

"How?" Valerie thought of the scraps she had found in Lucie's hand.

"No one knows."

"But the killings stopped when you started sacrificing animals to appease it," Valerie said. The cup of tea was heavy and hot in her hands.

"Yes, but it was after a long period of brutality. It was then that we started the bells. Those four tolls. Every month." She looked down, tears welling. "I thought those days were over."

There had been a time when Valerie had no understanding of the significance of those church bells.

We were five or six. I was on the outskirts of the town square, waiting for Peter. But he wasn't there.

"Watch your head!"

I looked up. Peter had climbed up the bell tower.

Angry that he'd thought of it before I had, I scrambled up the eaves of the church to meet him, refusing his help. We were so alike.

We were small enough to fit under the lip of the bell. Our own private world. No laws. In the brassy shade, Peter said, "Ring it."

"Just ring it?"

"Wolf death knell. Four times, four strokes."

Peter always brought out the best and the worst in me.

I grabbed the clapper and heaved it against the side of the bell.

Dong! Dong! Dong! Dong!

The chiming threw the village into chaos, fathers setting their jaws as they pushed past frantic and unhinged women, mothers counting their children as they ushered them to the tavern.

Peter and I jumped out from under the bell at the noise. Someone spotted us.

"The woodcutter's girl!"

I saw my mother searching for me down below, white with horror. I watched the shifting of her face from terror to disappointment to rage. My mother and father led me away from Peter, who kicked at the dust as the square emptied and the day's work resumed.

Now everything had changed. Valerie let herself sink into Grandmother's lap.

The middle of the night had arrived without their realizing it.

Valerie began tunneling into sleep, but she snapped awake at a noise.

Drip, drip, drip.

It was only a soaking wet rag hanging from a hook. Valerie breathed. Unprompted, floorboards shifted and creaked.

Grandmother saw that Valerie couldn't sleep. Night, she knew, was the time when dark thoughts tugged at the psyche like strings.

"Drink, darling."

"My sister is dead. . . ." Valerie said, trying to accept it.

"I know, dear. Drink a bit more."

The kettle was old, and it had left its iron taste in the tea.

Valerie felt her dry eyes becoming heavy and closed them, feeling the cool sting of her wet eyelids. She was thinking of Lucie's death, staring down at it, like something that waited at the other end of a tunnel.

"The Wolf killed Lucie. . . ."

She did not finish her thought, though, because sleep had taken her like death.

12

Inside the mountain, the boasting that had gone on in the tavern had given way to an anxious quiet.

"This way, men," Henry heard the Reeve whisper as they reached the fork, nodding toward a tunnel that descended into a den of darkness. The Reeve had turned to face the huddle of followers, with Peter and Henry standing firm on either side like bookends. Even with the light given off by the torches, the men's faces were cloudy in the inky black of the cave. The air smelled curdled, thick and sour.

"Not safe," muttered a leather worker without much conviction. "We can't see what's beyond the bend."

"We'll take the other fork," stated Peter, gesturing to his half of the group.

Henry looked at his father. They didn't want to admit it, but Peter was right. A group of twenty men was too many to maneuver in the dark cave. Henry wished he'd spoken up first.

"Yes," he said, just to have said something. "Some of us ought to split off."

"As you see fit," the Reeve declared arrogantly, walking on alone as the other men weighed the options, chose their sides. A few, glad for the Reeve's leadership, decided to follow. Peter, Henry, Adrien, those who wanted to lead rather than be led, were awkwardly left on their own. At least this way, Henry would be able to keep a close watch on Peter.

Henry hoped his father would leave it up to him, but Adrien, eyeing the assembled group, assumed control. The woodcutters were with them, staying on like burrs — they would go where Peter went. Cesaire, lagging behind as he went for one last enervating sip of his leather-bound flask, reluctantly decided that he would follow the Reeve's group and jogged to catch up.

On their own now, Adrien, Henry, Peter, and the woodcutters crept forward. The woodcutters tried to keep their footsteps light, but they were big and gruff and had never done much tiptoeing.

Henry sidled up next to Peter, startling him.

"It could get dangerous down here." He lit a match. "You'd better watch yourself."

"Watch *yourself*," Peter said, motioning to the flame that

had eaten its way down the length of the match. The threat his look held was evident even in the pitch dark.

"Right," Henry said, shaking his hand when the fire nicked him.

Before the rivalry could escalate, the group reached yet another fork. One branch was more menacing than the other, all pitch-black.

"We need to search every corner." Peter made a show of directing the woodcutters to separate themselves again. "We'll take the steep way."

"No," Henry cut in, eager to disagree and to keep Peter from making yet another decision for them. "We should stay together now."

"Maybe you should go home and wait for Father Solomon," Peter called over his shoulder, already on his way down the sloping path.

At the boys' clashing words, the woodsmen exchanged knowing glances. Did they want to entrust their lives to a prideful young boy? They looked back at Henry and Adrien silhouetted at the top, alone, indecisive, and hesitantly followed Peter. Peering after them, Henry felt his father's eyes on him. *Why had I not been the one to suggest it?*

Peter grinned broadly to himself, satisfied that he'd won. His group kept close behind him, the light from his torch roaming the walls and ground for any signs of movement.

Inching through a narrower passageway, the woodcutters were afraid, placing one cautious foot in front of the other, waiting for the Wolf to spring upon them, waiting to fall into the blackness of death. A soft breeze blew; a restless evil seemed to be rustling through the darkness.

A few moments later, a woodcutter, startled by a large protruding rock, dropped his bow. It echoed tinnily throughout the tunnels. The men were moved by mindless fears, but, luckily, Peter thought for them. *Walk*, he thought. *Wait for the air to change, to sense that moment of stillness* before *a movement is made.*

The air changed in one crushing instant, a forceful gust of wind stinging through the cave, shuttling him and his men into the chaos of nothingness.

Henry, far away, saw the walls disappear into a panic-filled cocoon of darkness as the gale of wind hit, stirring bits of earth and tossing grit into his eyes.

All he heard were shouts. Screams. Running feet.

His torch blew out.

The Reeve saw it first. That triangular smudge, the half circle of four round blots, and, worst of all, the four tiny ticks above. The Wolf's bloody print stamped into the dirt, spotlit by the Reeve's torch. He bent down over the ground, his men gathering around him, when, from somewhere deeper in the cave, he heard a faraway cry.

A man had been attacked.

The Reeve was ready for it, knew from the first pitch of the piercing noise exactly where it had come from.

"Run!" he shouted.

Most of the men followed, but a few scattered, racing away from the cry, headed for the mouth of the cave. Their screams echoed through the mountain.

Down the tunnel, down, down, the Reeve instructed himself. *Too far now for the fork to be the closest way through. Must be another way. The ground is no good here, the silt too loose. Careful not to slide. Don't trip over rocks on the edges of the path.*

His breath was loud and his feet louder. *There's some light. Run to the light, maybe something there.* He could see it now. *An opening, a chamber, up ahead!*

The Reeve stumbled into the space, his men trickling after him. Snow, painted red by the moonlight, swirled in from an opening in the rocks high overhead. Scanning the perimeter of the room, his eyes fell upon twisted, towering shapes.

Rock formations?

Inching closer, keeping a watchful eye out for movement, he went to them.

And saw that they were not rocks at all.

Bones, human bones. Piled as high as ten feet. They were

141

so sharply white that they looked almost painted. The Reeve stood before the tower, chastened.

He looked up. Where was the Wolf? *It couldn't have gotten out....* The empty eyes of the skulls stared him down, their mouths pulled into grins, mocking his plight but offering no answers.

Scanning the room . . . he came to something else.

Adrien. His body lay cold and lifeless, ripped up gruesomely by the Wolf.

Something heaved in the Reeve's chest. He felt the men's stunned silence behind him. He would find the Wolf and make it pay. With a surge of aggression, he did not step carefully now. He delighted in taking up space, in treading with a heavy, echoing step. He *would* find it.

Caught up in imagining the grandeur of his glory to come, the Reeve heard a noise behind him.

A low snarl.

He spun around and found himself face-to-face with a mouthful of angry fangs. Saliva gathering at the corners. Canines huge and gleaming.

Without knowing how it had happened, the Reeve saw his own dagger in his hand before him. The hair on the beast's neck bristled, and the noxious slaver from its horrible mouth dripped heavily onto the cave floor. Its eyes met his. Time stood still. And then the monster sprang, arcing toward its next victim.

13

ang!
    Valerie awoke from a place deep in a night-mare, her sweaty hair matted to her head even though the room was cold. The first morning light was blue-gray, the color of slate.

Valerie tried to orient herself. She wasn't in her own bed; she was at Grandmother's house—and her sister was dead. The noise had come from Grandmother's room.

"Grandmother?"

Valerie stepped barefoot through the house, feeling the cool air breeze up between the floorboards.

"Grandmother...?"

She was still in bed, facing away from Valerie, the covers pulled tightly over her willowy body. The edges of the peachy silk coverlet around her fluttered in the breeze. A shutter slammed against its frame. A window had been left open to the wind.

Or had someone come in?

Valerie moved to close it. Outside, the forest looked stooped and sad, the trees hunched in the snow.

She turned back to Grandmother, whose shape looked oddly elongated, stretched out, almost as if her limbs had been pulled from their sockets.

Valerie stepped closer. The figure stirred, then began to rise. Valerie shifted back, terrified, ready to run....

But it was only Grandmother, the old woman offering a smile as she blinked awake.

After swallowing a cold breakfast, Valerie hurried home through the woods wrapped in both her cloaks, old and new, to fend off the chilly air.

"Mother?" Valerie asked as she stepped into the cottage.

Suzette looked up. She was seated in a chair, her gaze fixed on the unlit fireplace. Desolate, grief-stricken.

Valerie's heart snagged. She should have stayed and waited with her.

"Is Papa...?" She didn't want to finish the question, because she didn't want to know.

"He's fine," Suzette said, looking at her hands. "The men have returned and are in the tavern."

Valerie nodded, unable to ask about Peter.

"You look beautiful," Suzette said, noticing the red cloak with tears in her eyes.

As Valerie turned to climb to the loft, her mother stood and grabbed her arm.

"Valerie, what's that on your wrist?" she asked, angling to see.

"It's nothing. A present from Henry." Valerie tried to conceal it, finding that she was embarrassed. She didn't want to be considered a woman yet, wasn't ready to be a recipient of jewelry from men. Nor did she want it to be noticed that she was wearing Henry's offering.

But it was almost more embarrassing to be embarrassed, and so she showed it. Her mother studied it for a long time.

"Valerie," Suzette said after a moment, "listen to me. Wear this bracelet. Don't take it off. You are a promised woman now."

Valerie nodded uneasily and climbed the loft ladder. In the safety of her own space, she changed her clothes. She marveled at her new red cloak, amazed again by its vibrant beauty.

Most cloaks were staid and wooly and made of stiff tweed. This cloak, however, was not starchy or scratchy. It was impossibly thin and almost fluid, as if it were a fabric of rose petals. It felt cool to the touch.

Feeling it against her bare arms and between her fingers, Valerie felt more powerful than ever before. There was something too natural about it, like another skin that had belonged to her all along. She felt strong and stealthy, and the cloak made her want to jump down from her loft into a panther crouch and run swiftly through the village, past the forest where it rained, into the fields where it didn't.

Stealing quietly past her mother, Valerie headed back out to the tavern.

The men, having returned from Mount Grimmoor without stopping home first, smelled spicy, like earth and sweat. Valerie could see the energy still pounding through their bodies. She walked around the edge of the crowd and leaned against a wall to listen.

As always at gatherings like these, Valerie sat apart, separate. A few of the villagers noticed her—the red cloak stood out, but she liked that. She felt safe in her red; from now on, she would always wear it.

The tavern was an archaeological site, containing the history of the village in its grime. Men had carved into the tavern walls since the day they'd been nailed together— initials, of course, but also spirals and faces and arrows and rabbits, serpents, clovers, interlocking circles, radiating crosses. The cushions in the booths were dirty, having provided comfort to so many different men. Massive beeswax candles oozed massive drops of wax onto the tables, cooling into hardened clots of butternut lava that often remained for months until some anxious drinker chanced to chip away at them with grimy nails. The deer skulls that hung along the far wall seemed to be smiling in death, as though they had taken a tantalizing secret with them.

Valerie scanned the room, saw her father and then Peter, beautiful in his heroic return, even though he didn't lift his head. Relief washed over her, and then anger. She hated that she cared so much, that she could still love someone who would not love her back....

But then she realized Henry was missing.

The Reeve was seated at the head of the table, surrounded by admirers, the Wolf's head skewered on a pike beside him. The men who had been in the caves—even the many who had fled—felt they had a right to share in his glory, that they had been necessary in his success. The Reeve was relaying the whole story, reenacting his tiptoe, then slamming down his mug at the climactic moment. Women gushed in admiration as the frothy beer dribbled down into his thick beard. Seeing his self-satisfied smile, Valerie was filled with contempt. The women hung on to his neck, praising him for his selflessness, for avenging that poor girl's death, when, really, that had nothing to do with it.

The tavern owner, a bald man with a crease running

from ear to ear at the back of his naked head, listened with rapt attention. His wife tended the bar as he sat, entranced. She had become large with child once and never recovered. The tavern owner himself, though, had no such excuse.

The Reeve finished his performance by bemoaning the loss they suffered, revealing the truth that was hanging in the air just out of Valerie's grasp. . . . Adrien had died for this glory. Valerie closed her eyes. She understood now why Henry wasn't here. There was some relief that it was the father, but also sympathy for the son who was now an orphan.

She looked over at Peter again, but he was still looking at the floor.

Everyone had come to the tavern because no one had wanted to go home. As the Reeve recounted his triumph, the town felt like rejoicing. A husband and wife were sharing a drink from the same huge cup. Two villagers sat together on a low bench next to the fire, enjoying the comfort of heat.

Someone was gutting the Wolf out in front of the tavern. Children looked on with horrified glee, shocked at their good fortune; their parents felt too complacent to remind them to stand back.

The sun rose high and shone brightly even as snow flurries continued to waft down, and the deaths, Adrien's and Lucie's, seemed almost justified for the freedom the villagers felt now. It didn't seem such an unfair trade, only two villagers over the last twenty years and now no more sacri-fices. It was validating to think that they could eat their fattest chicken themselves, that they could work outside well into dark, that nothing was off-limits, and that they could own their lives again.

They were glad to know, too, that money did not mean exemption, the richest man having been the one to go. They had been spared, and maybe it was because they'd deserved to be.

It seemed a small price to pay, those two deaths.

But the price was not small, Valerie thought.

Claude appeared at the window, fogging the blue glass as he made a funny face. He became blurry, though, as Valerie saw past him to something that was being wheeled by.

Adrien, his dead body lying atop the undertaker's cart.

Only his head was exposed, eyes closed in eternal sleep, never to open again. Blood had seeped slowly out of his body like syrup and become a blotch on the cloth.

Madame Lazar trailed behind, wailing her grief. Her eyes looked through the window to see Valerie, and they held her gaze until she'd passed the frame.

Men reached up with filthy hands, bringing their hats to their chests in respect as the body passed.

"To Adrien." Cesaire raised his glass, realizing that perhaps their carousing was in poor taste. "For his sacrifice."

"To Adrien!" The rest of the villagers raised their glasses.

151

Looking up first to see if Peter would notice, Valerie slipped out of the tavern. Henry had offered his condolences, and now she would, too. She didn't know what she would say, but she knew where he would be.

She stepped into the blacksmith shop. The door to the forge was open, a fiery cave, and its innards glowed red through the smoke. For a long while, Henry, his body half-bare as he threw vicious sparks, did not realize she was there. Valerie felt wretched that the pale, powerful torso reminded her of Peter's bare chest from the day before, and how warm it had been.

Valerie thought of the betrothal Suzette had arranged. She was even more trapped than she'd been before; there was no way she could run away now, abandoning Henry in his grief. She felt guilty, then, too, for even thinking of it.

Valerie knew that Adrien's body had been carried in, that it must have been lying cold in the loft above. She did not look up.

"Henry...your father was a brave man."

He continued attacking the metal with a sledgehammer, brutally hacking at the anvil. She wasn't sure he had heard her. Then he stopped short, the hammer hanging heavy in the air, the fire snapping in front of him.

"I was close enough to smell it," he seethed, not turning. "But I was afraid. I hid from it."

Clang!

"I should have done something."

Clang!

"I should have saved him."

Valerie saw that he was destroying all of their half-finished projects. They would remain that way forever.

"I've lost someone, too, Henry—I know how it is. Please, come away from the fire."

He didn't.

Clang!

"Henry, please."

One of the fiery specks spat out of the forge and landed on Henry's arm, searing his flesh. Punishing himself, he did not stop to remove it until finally, with one quick motion, he gestured violently toward the door, shaking it off.

"Valerie, leave," he snarled. "I don't want you to see me like this."

Knowing what it was like to want to be alone, she left, but she was unable to dispel the image of him, blackened with soot and angry in the red light of the forge.

Exiting the smithy, Valerie was surprised to find her mother sitting on a log. Bleary-eyed, Suzette was staring at the upper level of the shop, where Adrien's shrouded body lay. Valerie unnerved her by coming up from the side to take her hand. It was then that she saw that Suzette was holding something half-hidden, something that glinted in the light.

A beautiful hammered bracelet...

Identical to the one Henry had made for Valerie.

Confused, Valerie felt for hers. It was intact on her wrist.

Valerie reached out to touch the metal of her mother's bracelet.

Caught off guard, Suzette pulled away. "I was wondering about a hinge," she muttered before pivoting on her heel and hurrying away.

But Valerie followed.

Suzette began to speak but stopped when the words didn't come.

It was then that Valerie understood.

"Mother, you told me you loved someone else before you were married."

Suzette didn't answer, her silence speaking the words that she couldn't.

She walked faster through the square, and Valerie picked up her own pace. They passed two carpenters building a teepee of branches in which they would burn the body of the Wolf, passed the villagers spilling out of the tavern carrying the Wolf's head on its pike.

"Tell me who it was."

Suzette slowed, turning away. The words caught in her throat, not wanting to surface. "I think you already know."

154

"Tell me. I want you to say it." Valerie couldn't help it, the way she couldn't resist pulling at a loose piece of string until the cloth had unraveled.

Suzette was tearful. She chewed at her lip.

"I'm the child," Valerie spat out. "You're supposed to be my mother. The least you can do is say it."

"The man I loved was Adrien Lazar."

Hearing it said out loud, Valerie shivered. She thought of the images her mother must harbor of Adrien, the things he must have said, the words that would have reverberated in her mind ever since. How often had she thought of him? For she must have.

When Suzette's eyes had fluttered in sleep, had she been dreaming of him handing her the hammered bracelet, helping her with the clasp, reaching for her? Washing at the basin, her hands dragging a cloth up and down the ridged wood of the washboard, had she felt his hands on her? The mazelike way the mind works, some unknowable thing that she or Lucie did surely prompted a crystalline image of Adrien. Valerie tried to imagine the memories her mother had of her lover, those that she kept in a private box to which only she had the key. Things that only she and Adrien would ever know, but Adrien's half had disappeared in the caves at Mount Grimmoor.

Valerie felt her blood stop flowing. It couldn't be. And yet it could. It made sense.

The evidence had been there in plain sight, hidden only by a lack of scrutiny.

And, like the string unraveling, another suspicion came.

"Does Papa know?" Valerie asked, her voice sounding to her like someone else's.

"No." She looked imploringly at her daughter. "Promise me you won't tell him."

Suzette saw Valerie's face and calmed. She could see the lengths her daughter would go to in order to protect her father.

"But know this," she said, becoming very serious. "It wasn't that I *couldn't* love your father. It was just that I already loved Adrien."

Valerie was overtaken by a sense of sadness for her mother. She felt suddenly older, her childhood lost. She felt she had an overhead view of her mother's life, that it could be mapped and that she could see where the route had gone astray. She couldn't help feeling that her mother had made a bad choice in marrying her father.

Tears stung Valerie's eyes, regrets for her father, for her mother.

Before Valerie could respond, a dark, glittering carriage rushed past. It was sinister and elegant; it came from the outside world.

Father Auguste ran out of the churchyard and into the street, shouting.

"He has arrived!"

Easy there," the coachman growled at the horses, as the black carriage pulled to a sleek stop.

Valerie heard hooves thundering across the snowy ground as a dozen fierce-looking soldiers rode in atop powerful stallions, their weapons gleaming in the afternoon sun. A masked bowman was carried in by a majestic white steed. The man wore a heavy helmet and shouldered a massive crossbow. The fearsome band of men wheeled behind them a huge iron elephant and wagons filled with all their gear: weapons and books, scientific implements and equipment. The crudely rendered elephant was huge and blocklike with a snaky, curled trunk and menacing eyes. Valerie saw the other villagers wondering about its use; it did not seem right that these big men would bring a toy. She noticed a hinged door in its iron belly and shuddered.

Valerie saw her friends there, but before she could cross to them, the caravan had reached a halt in the square. She nodded at Roxanne, but Rose and Prudence didn't see her. Either that or they were holding her engagement against her.

The coachman looked a bit sick from the uneven road. It had been a long, fast journey, evidently, and the proud horses, with world-weary eyes, stamped out their frustrations. Their jingling bridles were the only sounds, as the crowd had already poured into the square and stood silently in anticipation.

Women peered down from porches and behind curtains, trying to see into the iron bars of the coach windows, which were molded into crosses. The tavern had emptied, and the men waited to see if the new arrival would live up to his reputation. Daggorhorn was a town accustomed to disappointment.

Peter stood far from Valerie. They did not look at each other. It was a good thing there was so much else to see.

She realized, though, that it might not be worth the risk. Hearing of her mother's secret woe, of the trauma wrought by love, Valerie didn't want to hurt like that. Love, desire— it was all so awful. She would forget Peter, she decided, and she would forget Henry. She would live a life in seclusion, live out in the woods like her grandmother, alone, self-sustained. Enough with "love."

A downtrodden village donkey clopped dejectedly out of

the way, probably thinking he'd rather have been a horse. Children had been depositing small items, acorns and corn-husk dolls, into the twin grooves the coach wheels had cleared in the snow. They scattered, though, when they looked up and saw the army that had assembled.

A few hulking men unloaded the coach, unstrapping wooden trunks and stacking them at the side of the road. The rest of the soldiers stood stock-still, awaiting orders. Even the monkey perched sharp-eyed on a pikeman's shoulder seemed to be awaiting a command.

"Presenting His Eminence..." a soldier said. He was a magnificent Moor, like no one Valerie had ever seen. His hair was cut close, so close it could have been drawn onto his skull, a shade of gray instead of black. He wore a two-handed sword slung coolly around his shoulders. His hands were huge, and looked capable of an easy throttling. He kept one hand on his side as he walked, resting easily on the coil of a black bullwhip. He was the Captain.

"...Father Solomon," a soldier who could only have been the Moor's brother finished. The two men spoke in a way that felt like velvet against skin.

The town marveled at Father Solomon's arrival. It was as impressive as royalty. Women smoothed themselves, their flyaway hair, their dingy skirts.

The onlookers held their breaths, waiting for the door to open. When it did, the townspeople were startled to see two small girls in the front-facing seats. They were so striking that the villagers almost forgot whom it was they were

161

watching for. No one had ever seen two little girls with such grief written so plainly on their faces.

Solomon was facing in, his erect back to the crowd.

"Please don't cry." He bent over them. "See all these children? See how scared they are?" He motioned to those gathered in the square. One little girl held on to a window bar as she peered out, her fingers wrapped in a tiny fist. "They are afraid because there is something evil here, a Wolf. And someone has to stop it."

Valerie liked the way Solomon spoke, accentuating each syllable as if every sound were a keepsake.

"Is it the beast that killed our mother?" the older girl asked, her cadence like a grown woman's. The girls looked rumpled from travel, from slumping down in those great leather seats until they were shoulder to shoulder. Solomon, though, did not look ragged or worn. When he turned, the crowd saw he was in impeccable, shining silvery armor, his windswept hair fiercely silver to match. He looked exactly as a Wolf slayer should.

"It may very well be," Solomon replied gravely, a darkness crossing his face.

The girls shuddered; the thought of the beast trumped any girlhood claim to Daddy's attention.

He held out his arms. They hugged him, and he bent down stiffly to kiss each girl on the head. He softened as he touched the back of his hand to the younger girl's hair.

"It's time." He nodded to the Captain. A shadowy figure

leaned forward to pull the sobbing girls into the dark interior of the coach. Their guardian.

"Be good, now," he said, shutting the door with a fatherly firmness. They would be safe in there. Valerie found that she was perversely jealous of Solomon's two little girls, safe behind their iron bars.

Father Solomon watched them go as the coach rolled out of the square and then out of the village altogether, whisking the girls off to a safer place. The villagers envied them, wishing they, too, could run off, be patted on the head or chucked under the chin. Father Solomon took a moment, steeling himself for work, before turning to the crowd, who had begun to feel that they were in the presence of a great leader. In his elegant black gloves and his velvet cape, purple like the king's, he was regal and commanding. The crowd knew from his face that he had seen a world they never would.

Realizing that it was their turn for his prized attention, Father Auguste stepped forward to speak for Daggorhorn.

"This is indeed an honor, Your Eminence." He bowed before the older man, the man who was so magnanimous as to stand before them in their humility. Valerie wanted to run her fingers over the soft fabric of his cloak, which caught the light as it fell across his shoulders.

Solomon nodded slightly. His motions were tight and complete.

"Fortunately, we were traveling through this region

already and were able to get here quickly. I understand that you have lost a village girl." He paced in front of the crowd. "Who in attendance is the girl's family?"

Suzette didn't move, and Valerie didn't see her father— he was probably still inside the tavern. Villagers shuffled. Glancing at Peter, who offered nothing from far across the crowd, Valerie resignedly raised her hand.

Solomon strode over to her and lowered her hand to rest in his. He smelled like oiled metal, like security.

"Do not worry," he said humbly with a bowed head. "Enough horrors have been witnessed, enough suffering endured. We will find the beast that killed your sister. I am sorry for your loss."

Even though she knew it was all theatrics, there was a certain comfort in it, in a public apology, in an acknowledgment that she, Valerie, was the one who had suffered.

He bowed slightly, his tender face hardening as he turned back to the men and women who had lost no one yet.

Valerie saw the Reeve swagger forward, unable to contain himself any longer. Valerie was disgusted by him and the other men; they were like children, with their violence and their vanity.

"You and your men are late." He set a great hand on Father Solomon's shoulder. "But you have arrived in time to take part in our festival." The tavern owner murmured support as the Reeve motioned to the furry head on the pike, its eyes glazed over, filmy and white.

"As you can see, the Wolf has been dealt with."

Father Solomon glanced down at the Reeve's hand, at his fingernails ringed with dirt. He stepped out from beneath its anchoring hold.

"That is no werewolf," Father Solomon muttered cryptically, shaking his head.

Valerie saw Roxanne and Prudence look at each other, and then they looked across at her. She shrugged in reply. Rose missed the exchange, still transfixed by the scene before her.

"Not anymore, it isn't," the Reeve said, meeting with approval from the crowd. "Maybe it doesn't look like a *were*wolf now, but you didn't see it when it was alive."

Daggorhorn men nodded in affirmation.

"You're not listening," Father Solomon said quietly, in a way that made everyone listen. "That is not the head of a werewolf."

There was a beat as the crowd tried to make sense of this. Was he joking, some high-class humor they didn't understand?

"No disrespect, Father, but we've lived with this beast for two generations. Every full moon, it takes our sacrifice." The Reeve's broad smile was buried in his thick beard. "We know what we're dealing with."

"No disrespect," Father Solomon countered, unwavering, "but you have *no idea* what you're dealing with."

Valerie was intrigued. Someone dared to question the Reeve—this was new.

"I see your denial. I was the same way once," Father

165

Solomon admitted, hesitating. "Let me tell you a story—my first encounter with a werewolf. I will think back to the night I would do anything to forget."

Valerie felt the crowd hold their breath.

"My wife's name was Pénélope. She gave me two beautiful daughters, as you have seen. We were a happy family, living in a village much like this one. And like Daggorhorn, ours was also plagued by a werewolf."

Solomon walked in front of his audience, his boots falling heavily.

"It was six autumns ago. The night was still, almost dead. The moon hung full overhead, casting its glow on everything. My friends and I left the tavern late at night after some...revelry."

Valerie saw him smile to himself, remembering, a smile that hinted at other, untold stories.

"We decided to hunt the Wolf. The thought that we might actually find it never occurred to us. But we did. And it proved to be fatal," he said with an exaggerated candor. "I came face-to-face with the beast. It breathed—I could feel it. It blinked—I could hear it. Energy coursed through me. I *trembled* with it."

Valerie found herself as caught up in the story as everyone else was. Even her mother listened intently at her side.

"But the Wolf let me go, turning instead to my friend and making me watch as he was ripped in half. Quickly. But not so fast that I didn't hear his spine snap."

Valerie felt sick, thinking of Lucie, of what she might have heard had she been there.

"I screamed, *like a woman*, and then it was on me. All I saw were yellow teeth. I hacked at it with my axe, and in a moment it was gone. I had cut off one of its front paws. Thinking it would make a clever souvenir, I took it home." He spoke intimately, as though he hadn't told any of this before.

"I arrived home, drunk and stumbling, exultant and proud. When I entered the front hall, I followed drops of blood like a trail to a black form lying on our kitchen table. Dark liquid was dripping off the edge and pooling onto the floor planks." The words had a physical effect on Solomon, his eyes glowing. "As I got closer, I realized with horror that it was my wife. A bloody rag was tied around her left wrist. Her hand was severed. And when I opened my sack, *this* was in its place." He paused, building up the suspense.

The Captain pulled a box from behind his back. He'd anticipated this moment. He marched up to the Reeve, coming too close, almost gratuitously so, and opened the box slowly, with a climactic flourish. The other villagers crowded in closer to look.

The velvet-lined box held a woman's mummified hand, wedding band glinting, lying atop a bed of petals. Children gasped and ran away, then hurried back for another look.

"Roses," Solomon cut in, "were Pénélope's favorite."

The villagers looked eagerly, some even taking a step forward.

"I told my girls that the werewolf had killed their mother. But that was a lie," he said in a voice that was ghostly still. "*I* killed her." Father Solomon's words hung in the air. "Because she *was* the Wolf. Do any of you know what it's like to kill the person you love most?"

He looked up at a sea of blank faces.

"You may soon. When a werewolf dies," Solomon began, "it returns to its human form."

He glanced at the wolf head, which had certainly lost some of its luster since he had begun his tale.

"That's just a common gray wolf. Your *were*wolf is still alive." He crossed himself. The first act was over. "Come now. To the tavern."

When everyone who could fit had filed in, Solomon held out a silver, gem-encrusted sword bearing an engraved image of Christ on the cross.

Seeing it, Father Auguste's eyes lit up. "This..." He steadied himself. "This is one of only three silver swords blessed by the Holy See. May I touch—?"

Solomon cast him a reproachful look.

Father Auguste stepped back, chastened.

"This is a very dangerous time," Solomon told the people

of Daggorhorn, who were held in thrall. Claude lay on his stomach in the rafters, overlooking the scene. Valerie smiled up at him briefly from where she stood, packed in, barely able to see. She wished she had thought to climb up there.

"Of course, you know what the blood moon means."

Didn't they? Everyone looked around for someone older to speak up.

"I see you have no idea what it means." His lips were tight.

The villagers felt their cheeks flush hot with embarrassment; they didn't like that.

"The orrery." Solomon held out his hand. It was all he had to do.

The Captain set onto the table a brass instrument fitted with round glass bulbs.

"The Persians invented it, but this one I made myself. Every little gear," he said, twirling a globe with one gentle finger, adjusting the position of another. He lit a candle, casting the model in a scarlet glow. "See, the red planet converges with the moon once every thirteen years. This is the *only* time a new werewolf can be created." With a snap of his wrist, the bulb exploded. They blinked at the sound.

Solomon smiled that tight little grin of his.

"During the week of the blood moon, the werewolf may pass his curse on with a single bite. Even in daytime—"

"Pardon me, but you're wrong." The Reeve looked pleased. "Sunlight makes a werewolf human—"

"No, it is you who are wrong," Solomon said, meeting the glares of the men who'd risked their lives in the caves. Father Auguste's eyes shone.

The Reeve shifted his stance.

"A werewolf is never truly *human* no matter how it appears. During a normal full moon, a Wolf bite will kill you. But during the days of the blood moon, your very *souls* are in danger."

The room chilled.

"For how long, exactly?"

"Four days."

Two nights are left, Valerie thought. *Tomorrow will be the final day.*

"As I've said," the Reeve interjected authoritatively, smiling, his jowlish cheeks pulling out to either side, "none of this matters. We're safe now. The Wolf is dead. I killed it myself in its lair, the cave at Mount Grimmoor." The Reeve began to turn, hoping that would be the end of it.

Solomon looked at him as though he were a child. The villagers were unsure which patriarch should receive their allegiance.

"You've been deceived by this beast." Solomon systematically cracked his knuckles. "Right from the start. Most likely, it lured a hungry wolf to the cave and trapped it there for you to find. It fooled you into thinking it lived on Mount Grimmoor so that you wouldn't look for it in the most obvious place."

He paused, letting them understand their own folly.

"The Wolf lives right here. In this village." He looked at the villagers. "Among you. It is *one of you*."

Starting at one end of the crowd, he met the eyes of every villager down the line. The masked bowman scanned the throng alongside him, his crossbow slung across his back.

"The real killer could be your neighbor. Your best friend. Even your wife." His eyes were like cut gemstones.

Valerie saw men thinking back to the cave. Who had been missing? It was impossible to know, in the chaos of the dark. Her own eyes crossed Madame Lazar's, Peter's, her parents'. She began to replay her friends' stories of what had happened at the campout in her mind. How was it possible that they had lost sight of Lucie? Had one of them held her back and dragged her away into the dark . . . or written a note to lure her out?

Her suspicious gaze settled on the people she had known her whole life. Then she realized they were staring right back at her.

"Barricade the village," Father Solomon commanded. "Post men at every gate along the town wall. No one leaves until we kill the Wolf."

The Reeve rubbed his teeth with his tongue.

"The Wolf is dead," he growled. "Tonight we *celebrate*."

Solomon stared at him, his eyes lit up like fire.

"Go ahead and celebrate," he said, throwing up his hands as only a man who was used to being listened to would. "We'll see who's right."

He turned and strode out of the tavern.

Father Solomon was a brisk walker, and Valerie had to run to catch up with him. But she stopped short as his back stiffened and his hand went for his sword. *Not a man to approach suddenly.*

He turned, and the menace drained from his eyes.

"I'm sorry," she said.

"No, no. What is it, child?"

"I need to know...my sister..."

"Yes?"

"Why? Why has the Wolf waited until now to attack? And why her?"

"Only the Devil knows."

He could see she wasn't satisfied, that she was not a simpleminded village girl who could be deterred by pious platitudes.

"Go speak with my scribe. He can show you things that will help you understand the unfathomable."

She dropped back as he strode onward.

"The unfathomable, yes," came an unfamiliar voice. "Understand, probably not."

She turned, and the scribe, who had been following Solomon, stopped and held out a leather-bound tome. He had an underbite and a kind face. Valerie inspected the clasp of the book. It felt like it was made of horse hooves, and it might have been. She didn't ask.

She opened the book with a *clack*. The images were beautifully rendered pencil drawings of the beasts Father Solomon and his men had slain.

The scribe fitted his spectacles onto his nose. Neat handwriting crawled steadily across the pages.

"That's the obour. Survives off blood and milk. Tears the udders off cows in the night." The scribe had a shuffling, breathy voice. "You don't want to come across one of those in your pantry."

She leafed through, noting the careful, elegant lines, the surfaces of the pages smudged with lead from having been touched and gone over many times. She ran her own fingers gingerly over the fantastical images.

"Beautiful, eh?"

"Yes."

"Things that haunt your dreams."

The pages were vellum with red and blue underlines surrounded in flowery gold, depicting strange creatures with crow heads, sea monsters with the bodies of lizards and the faces of men perched atop towering letters and breathing out red smoke. She could not bring herself to believe they were real.

But her heart caught when her eyes fell on a hulking image of a bipedal werewolf. She thought of sweet Lucie and closed the book, unable to look any longer.

15

hat remains of my sister will soon be no more, Valerie thought as she walked down the sloping path to the river. It was late afternoon now, and Cesaire was carrying one end of the thin raft that held Lucie's body, Valerie and Suzette the other. They reached the shore, where the dirt was too soft and felt like ash shifting beneath the snow. It was scattered slightly with the faint tracks of feet and paws that preceded theirs.

They saw that the Lazars—what was left of them— were already there, standing vigil over Adrien's body, lying on its own raft. Madame Lazar stood stiffly upright, as if the older woman refused to stoop. Henry stood behind her.

They both nodded as Valerie and her family approached. Henry raised his eyebrows at Valerie, silently apologizing for how he'd acted at the smithy. They set Lucie's raft beside Adrien's. The sight made Valerie glance at her mother, but Suzette was lost in her silent double sorrow.

Cesaire squatted and began preparing the two torches, sparking the flint, assessing the river.

Valerie couldn't help feeling like her father's sadness was unbearable.

Valerie stood back near the woods. A great tree had been swept over in the previous night's wind, and its upturned roots clutched at the air for its lost ground.

Cesaire looked up; the torches were ready.

Henry stepped down the uneven bank, receiving a torch. Before he could think about it for too long, he pitched it onto Adrien's raft and helped the floating coffin into the river, which rippled like smoke-colored silk. Its cuts and swells met always in the same furrows and creases, so that it looked at one moment just the same as the next. It seemed the water wasn't moving at all. It would douse the flames, but only after the fire had finished what it had been called upon to do.

Henry moved to his grandmother as the flames took hold of the raft, standing to her side, rolling a pebble back and forth with his foot. Madame Lazar closed her drapelike eyelids, and Valerie could see the tears threatening to brim over. For a moment she was just a mother who had loved her son. Valerie felt that she was glimpsing the older woman's olive pit heart.

Valerie could not imagine Madame Lazar as a young girl, someone reliant on another. It was hard to believe that she participated in such human necessities as sleeping and eating. And yet, Madame Lazar was not all bad. Valerie, who had explored everywhere, knew that, privately, the woman left bowls of milk out for stray dogs.

Through the haze of grief, the five mourners heard the sound of feet scuffing through pebbles. It was Claude, who'd come to pay his respects to Lucie. Catching Valerie's eye, he moved down the bank. He was coping as best he could. Claude had believed in many things, and yet before that day, he had not believed in evil. It had taken seeing Lucie lying dead in the wheat field to convince him.

Evil was everywhere.

Madame Lazar sniffed and turned away from the intruder, but Valerie offered Claude a small smile. She didn't mind that he came to join the family in their grief.

Cesaire, seeing that Adrien's raft was well out into the river, stepped forward. Valerie shook her head. One more moment.

Valerie took in her sister for the last time—her flesh, those small feet that did not seem ready to disappear forever. She looked and tried to say good-bye.

But good-bye was not easy.

Suzette moved to the raft, trembling with tears. *Mothers should not outlive their children*, Valerie thought. *Nature should have a law against that.*

Looking first for permission, Cesaire touched the torch to the edge of the raft. Once it had caught, he delivered it into the river.

Suzette hovered behind him, far enough back that it was clear they were not grieving separately but also not together.

Valerie felt a touch, and she turned instinctively into Henry's chest. A quiet place. She felt an arm around her, and Valerie realized she was crying, wetting his leather collar with her tears. When she looked up, Madame Lazar had disappeared.

As the flames settled to meet the river, Valerie stepped away from the shelter of Henry's body. Not wanting to go to her mother, nor feeling she should go to her father, she walked along the skirt of the river, the surface marbled like unmixed batter. Her sister was now water, cool and clear. She found a place where the river lapped gently at the shore, where a few plants stood up through the snow. How could it be that plants still grew? She sat, letting the cold, biting tide shock her as it washed over her feet, rinsing them, until Claude called for her, the wind carrying his voice.

Turning, she saw her mother watching the two rafts, wondering why she hadn't been taken, too.

Lucie was gone—there was no doubt about that now.

Valerie and her parents walked home together, following the dark tree line along the village wall. Entering through a reinforced barricade, they passed under the relentless glares of Father Solomon's soldiers patrolling on horseback. The soldiers ate as they watched, their weapons slung across their bodies. Out of the sides of their mouths, they took yanking bites of massive loaves or tossed back mugs of ale in two great gulps, but they did not take their eyes off the family.

The newly erected barricade was frightening; it meant that now the world was just the village against the Wolf. But it frightened Valerie for a reason that she was afraid to admit, even to herself.

The barricade meant that she would be trapped inside.

It didn't even matter to her where the Wolf was, she realized in a moment of clarity. What mattered was that there was an outside and that she was not a part of it. She felt like she was way down at the bottom of a well and that someone at the top was closing the hatch.

Through the dark, the family of three heard a deafening noise, and then something jumped out of the bushes at them, surreal and terrifying.

It was a wolf with a man's face.

The man in the wolf costume jangled Valerie's nerves, already raw. She'd almost forgotten that the Reeve's "celebration" was still happening. Wandering into the square with her senses heightened, she felt eyes staring up at her. Afraid, she looked to her left and saw that they belonged to a boar's head being carried by on a pewter platter. It had a blushing apple in its mouth and grapes for eyes, which gave it a faraway look.

A towering effigy of the Wolf had been built from a pyramid of roots, sharpened sticks, and debris. It burned at the far end of the square, coughing out sparks from its blackening mouth. The blood moon hung ripe in the void-like sky.

A stage had been cobbled together out of a few sagging

planks, upon which the goat herder and a few woodsmen were cranking hurdy-gurdies and strumming lutes. Simon, the tailor, had gotten his hands on a bagpipe, and the thing wheezed shrill and loud, like a dying animal. The musicians blew as hard as they could into their horns, running out of breath, gulping down more before beginning again.

Despite all the delicious-looking food, wafts of rotten garbage and men's sweat still filled the square. Valerie felt her stomach turn.

She looked for Solomon and his men but did not see them. She had noticed their camp set up in the expansive barn behind the granary and figured they must be holed up there now, refusing to participate.

Everyone seemed to be celebrating all the harder to convince themselves that they should be celebrating at all. They danced, frantic and wild, so that they would forget in the frenzy. A few men, respectable by day, lumbered around on all fours, ruining their pants in the snow. A woman tripped into the mud in front of Valerie, but before she could help her up, she had already been yanked into a dance. Red-faced men swung their heavyset partners, admiring their wives' curves from an arm's length, hands joined overhead. Sisters danced with their younger brothers but held their eyes fixed on the boys across the stage. Voices ricocheted across the square, making it seem like hundreds more people were there.

Surrounded by everyone she knew, Valerie felt completely alone.

Suzette kept her eyes down and melted into the crowd without a word. Valerie saw the Reeve, his bald head shiny with sweat, lording over the scene at a long table set up in front of the tavern. He beckoned for her to join, but she ignored him out of contempt. It was difficult, though, to maintain her embittered sense of outrage. There were too many people caught up in the delirium of the celebration to lay the blame on one particular person. It was exhausting to be grief-stricken. Valerie gave up.

Her father, already hanging carelessly off a branch, blew fast and hard into an ox horn, pointlessly signaling the beginning of the festival that people had already begun. The horn sounded long and low, like someone blowing his nose.

"Hey! Hey! Everybody!"

Valerie and the people nearby turned to face the shrill voice. Marguerite had grabbed a rusty overturned bucket to boost her own height and was clamoring to get atop, lifting her arms above her head. "Quiet, all!" The would-be podium rested on a slant and began to give way backward. Henry caught it to stabilize the barmaid before she fell.

Those at the ends of the table continued carrying on, either not hearing her or not bothering to listen. Marguerite raised a pewter mug. "To the Reeve!" Then, realizing she had commanded everyone's attention, she added, "For, uh, his bravery and his courage and his fearlessness."

Valerie wondered whether she was going to say something more. It seemed Marguerite herself wasn't sure, not having known what she was going to say in the first place.

"And for ... killing that Wolf dead as doornails. Like the nails made by little Henry."

Henry smiled, trying to steady his face into politeness.

"Though he's not so little anymore." She winked at him, wagging her hips for emphasis. Though they were both bright shades of pink, Claude and Roxanne, standing off to one side together, graciously said nothing. This was not the first time their mother had embarrassed them. Valerie gave Roxanne a sympathetic glance.

Valerie hung back from the crowd. Feelings of pain and fear flooded the villagers and mixed with rage, making them feel invincible and savage. Nightfall always made them feel lawless.

A candlemaker, sitting along the edge of the well, kicked with his feet, drenching the musicians. The mandolin player peered into his sound hole.

Prudence stole up to Valerie, the hem of her gray skirt clutched in each fist as she danced.

"I'm so glad you came!" she called over the noise, letting her brown hair swish from side to side. Valerie hoped this meant she was forgiven for being betrothed to Henry. She decided to confide her concern to her friend.

"Prudence, the Wolf's not gone, is it?" Valerie asked, her voice sounding hollow in her own ears as she asked the question that burned and died in everyone's throats, like a spent firecracker.

Prudence stopped dancing and let her skirt fall.

"Why would you say something like that?" She frowned. "You heard the Reeve."

"But Father Solomon—"

"The men know what they're doing. Now, come on!"

Valerie saw Claude's red hair standing out from the whirling mob. She hoped that he would be able to have some fun after the events of the day before.

Seeing that Valerie was watching, he attempted an animated jig, kicking his legs out at odd angles to make her laugh. She forced a smile for him. However, not realizing his own size, the dance swung him into a group of grouchy women, who had to back reluctantly out of his way. He was smiling sunnily at them when a teenage boy, William, ran by and swooped the hat off Claude's head.

"Who's afraid of the big, bad wolf?" William called out in mocking innocence.

"*Stop!*" Valerie yelled, but the kid was already headed too far in the other direction.

Claude ran after him, chasing him around the well. He skittered in the dirt as he tried to follow. Roxanne, who never lost sight of him for long, hurried over, shrugging meekly at Valerie as she comforted her brother.

Who is everyone pretending for? Valerie wondered. Near the Wolf effigy, a couple of half-wits were throwing

185

broken furniture into the bonfire. The crowd whooped as someone raised the full moon sign from the Wolf altar above his head and smashed it into the fire.

She saw that Henry Lazar was making his way toward her along the edge of the square. She thought of the refuge she had found with him earlier and, oddly, felt no desire to avoid him.

"Henry," she said, feeling the bond of grief.

"This all seems so wrong. They're barely in their graves," Henry said. Surveying the raucous mob, Valerie was horrified to see Rose swaying against Peter, seductively grinding her broad hips. He held her close to him, clutching her to his chest as they rolled their shoulders against each other in unison.

"No," Valerie said, suddenly turning on Henry, the compassion she'd felt for him inexplicably reaching its limit. "Let them celebrate."

"Now hardly seems the time." He shook his head.

Suddenly, feeling the depth of her own hurt, she wanted to hurt him.

"You heard the Reeve. The Wolf is dead. Let's all get back to our lives." She instantly hated herself. He had voiced exactly what she'd felt, and she'd attacked him for it. Valerie didn't feel she was in her right mind.

She turned to apologize, but he'd already disappeared.

William ran by, wearing Claude's hat. Valerie saw Claude was again hanging back, around the square, still embarrassed and unsure of what to do. It had been a hard night for him. She moved to his side.

"William's an ass. We'll get your hat back."

Trying hard not to seem childish, he couldn't help stammering, "M-my sister made it."

Valerie patted his arm and looked after William, anywhere but at Peter. She turned her eyes to the fire. As the music got louder, the flames heaved higher and higher into the night sky. Then Valerie saw that her father had slipped in the mud and was unable to get up. A girl leapt over him, the ribbons on her boots rudely grazing his face.

"Excuse me, Claude." As she approached, she saw that a man in a ratty wolf costume was standing over Cesaire, beating him with his flat tail, blowing in his face.

"I'll huff and I'll puff and—"

"Get off him!" Valerie shouted.

When he didn't, Valerie ran over, grabbed a firewood log, and fiercely whacked him with it. A few women quieted their taunting and stepped back, impressed.

"I said get *off*!" she shouted, too loud over the music. The man scampered back into the howling crowd.

"Blow my eardrum out, why don't you?" Cesaire laughed from the ground, his face hugging the mud, apparently unaware of what had happened to him. Cesaire had clearly seen the night as an occasion to drink as much as he could, whatever he could, until he was too inebriated to get his hands on anything else.

"I'm serious." Usually, Valerie put up with his merrymaking. But tonight, she couldn't do it. With all the heightened attention on the family, she wanted to get him safely

187

inside. At the moment, Valerie felt the loss of Lucie more acutely than she had yet; Lucie would've helped her take care of their father.

Valerie saw, with shame, that he was lying in a pool of his own vomit.

"Papa…"

"I'm getting up, I'm getting up."

He managed to sit up, but he couldn't go any farther.

"I think I chipped off a bit of tooth," Cesaire noted from his seat, rubbing his cheek.

Valerie helped to ease him onto his unsteady feet. He was drunk and trying very hard. She held both his hands as he rocked back and forth, trying to balance his weight.

"The things that seem so easy in the day…"

Valerie let him lean on her as she dragged him away from the crowd and pointed him toward home.

He looked down at his shirt, at the vomit.

"Just flick this off and I'll be fit to see the king," he said, attempting a flick.

They passed a group of teenagers.

"Did the bearded lady faint?" a teenager called out in a lilting voice.

"Damsel in distress!" sang another.

Valerie's jaw clenched. She felt the weight of her father like a stone around her neck.

"Don't worry about them, Valerie," Cesaire muttered.

As he lurched along beside her, Valerie was ashamed for

feeling ashamed of him. She knew he was aware of it, and she knew it hurt him.

"You're my good girl," he got out, getting teary-eyed, fragile in his drunken state. He tried to pat her with his free arm but missed.

He turned and this time managed to find Valerie's head. She knew he needed to get away from the infernal wreckage of the festival, a celebration in spite of his daughter's death.

He looked around, wondering where home was, finding it.

He jerked free of her.

"…gwanback havfun," he commanded her. It was all the fatherly wisdom he could muster. And without so much as a glance more in her direction, he floundered onward, looking like maybe he ought to have a little rest under the house before attempting the ladder.

Making her way back to the square, Valerie saw two little girls arm in arm, careful not to lose each other in the crowd. Valerie thought of a festival her family had gone to when she and Lucie were young girls, whirling around in their father's arms, and later, their mother reaching down to feed bite-size pieces of meat into their mouths, as though they were baby birds.

"I wish I could feel as free as Rose does." Prudence sashayed up to her, shouting over the music, maintaining her perfect posture even as she danced.

Already knowing to what she was referring, Valerie turned uneasily to face Peter and Rose. She was reaching around and wrapping her hands around his neck. He held his hands to her face and reached into her dark hair that was similar to his own, which was somehow more intimate, a deeper betrayal, than whatever their bodies were doing. The band played, whooping and jeering every so often at the pair, which was only fuel for Rose to grind harder. Peter kept his head down. She felt like Rose was punishing her for Henry—which hadn't even been Valerie's choice.

Valerie wished they would die. She couldn't decide which one she hated more, Peter or Rose. Her vision blurred as she watched them.

"Are you all right?" Prudence asked, her hand on Valerie's back.

"Yes."

"I wonder if we should stop her. She's ruining whatever's left of her reputation dancing with *him*." Prudence pushed a strand of brown hair behind her ear.

Valerie saw that the bonfire had grown. The flames shot up high and sent elongated shadows dancing across the ground.

"No," she said darkly. "Let her do what she wants."

Just then, a glass worker passed by guzzling ale, barely

recognizable beneath the mess of leaves pasted onto his face.

Valerie reached for the man's bottle and, leaning back, let the spicy brew meet the tip of her tongue with a surge. She let the whole of the bottle's contents burn down the back of her throat. Looking up, Valerie felt she was swimming through the air.

She grabbed Prudence and pulled her into a wild dance, the two girls lit up by the ecstatic flames.

They leaned forward, keeping their legs wide. Facing each other, they dipped down, letting their long hair spin out around them as they came up. Two stomps forward, one stomp back. Then three stomps forward, so that they were eye to eye, chest to chest. Never having given much thought to her body, Valerie was more free than Prudence and the other girls, and she shook like she was inhabited by a powerful spirit.

Valerie and Prudence didn't think about which way to turn, or about which way the other would. They just did it, and it worked. Loose-limbed, they spun in rapturous circles, and they lifted up their skirts and floated their hands to meet each other's. They stared each other down, and their eyes shone with secrets. Valerie felt exhilarated with the communion she and her friend shared.

Meanwhile, Peter hovered over Rose, his body resting on hers as she flared her skirt, showed her legs. Though Valerie and Peter were dancing differently, their bodies moving in different ways, they were both doing the same dance. It was a jealousy dance, old as the human race.

Catching glances threaded through the whirring bodies of a couple who danced between them, Valerie watched Peter watching her, both pretending not to. The energy flowed between them, carried by the lines of vision that made sure never to meet.

Slam!

Without Valerie realizing it, Henry had come stumbling toward her, ale spilling sloppily out of his cup, clearly the latest in a long string of drinks. Peter had moved protectively to block Henry's path.

She felt some satisfaction that Peter must have been as aware of her as she had been of him.

Working hard to make sense of things through his blur of drunkenness, Henry finally realized that it had been Peter. He whipped around, breathing heavily, heading straight for his rival, pushing a drunken trio of masked piggy men out of the way.

Seeing the wild look in Henry's eyes as he charged, Rose moved aside to cling to Prudence. Henry shoved Peter hard enough that he staggered backward.

"Take it easy, friend," said Peter, regaining his balance, quickly understanding the condition Henry was in.

"*Friend?* You left us. In the caves." Henry's muscles tensed.

Peter stepped back cautiously. Henry didn't look like himself.

"Seems someone can't hold his drink," Peter said. He didn't go further, sensing then that Valerie might be thinking of her father.

"And now," Henry continued on his own track, stepping closer to meet him, the smell of alcohol on his breath, "my father, too, is *dead*."

Valerie moved to Henry. "Please, don't do this," she said, stepping in. "It's not worth it."

Henry pushed past her, not realizing his own weight. The force knocked her back. Peter grabbed Henry's arm and twisted it. Overreacting, Henry reared back his fist and landed a punch in the hollow of Peter's eye. The crowd laughed as Peter fell hard to the ground.

Henry scrambled on top of him, held him by the collar, forced Peter to face him as he'd never done. He looked into the eyes of the man he wanted to blame for his parents' deaths, because it was a shelter from the terrible thought that everything could be lost to a simple slip of fate. "You filth," he spat out.

This really got the villagers going. But Peter didn't laugh. He pulled a knife from his boot and leapt up, thrusting it viciously in Henry's face.

"Keep your hands off her or I'll cut them off." The knife shivered in front of Henry, inches from his face, Peter looking as if he might cut them off anyway.

Henry, ready to take him, did not look afraid.

"Peter, please..." Valerie said softly. Henry was looking for a boyish tumble, but Peter, she knew, was out for blood.

193

Valerie's voice caught as she was struck with the fierce beauty of it, of being loved that much. She thrilled with guilt and pride at the thought of her own power, at the thought of being loved murderously.

Hearing her voice, Peter backed away slowly but stopped to direct the knife at Henry once more. "You *will* be sorry for this." Then he disappeared from the square.

Henry stood mute as Valerie glanced at him for a moment in disappointment before turning to run after Peter.

She followed him into the dark shelter of an alley. The enclosed space dampened the noise of the festival to a murmur.

Peter waited against a wall, chest heaving, eyes wild and dangerous.

"Leave me alone."

But she felt too powerful for that. She would not be told what to do.

"You're bleeding." She reached up to tenderly touch his eye.

"So what?" he said, brushing her hand aside roughly. "Jesus, Valerie. What's the matter with you? What do I have to do to make you stop?"

Valerie wouldn't take no for an answer, because she knew how wonderful yes would be. Although Valerie had sworn off her feelings for him earlier, she could not deny what now felt so real. She felt the drink coursing through her, carrying her on its tide.

"Peter," she began. He looked up at her, and she could see the pain in his eyes. "I love you," she said freely. With Peter, she was laid bare; he extracted her from herself.

Peter didn't know what to say. His eyes glimmered, bright and burning. He only let her see them a moment before he turned away. He took in a ragged breath.

"What were you doing with Rose anyway?" she demanded, asking a lot of him.

Peter darkened again. He turned his back to her, took a step farther into the alley, and said in a dead voice, "I don't have to like her to get what I want."

"I don't believe you," Valerie said, reaching for his face again. Peter pulled away from her. "You're lying."

Valerie wanted to touch him so badly, to feel the beat of his heart, to know that it was in there, that this was her Peter. Before he could stop her, she'd swiftly wrapped her arm around him from behind and laid her hand to his chest. She said, "Your heartbeat is so fast. I know you feel the same way."

Spinning around, he grabbed at the bracelet Henry had given her. She didn't let him have it.

"Valerie, you know I can't give you anything like that. I can't now, and I never will."

"You think I care about his money?"

"Valerie," he said, giving her another chance to back out, "I'm wrong for you."

195

"So what?"

He finally turned to face her, daring to believe, and she suddenly found herself kissing him on his soft lips, full and fast. He hesitated, struggling with his promise to her mother, and yet as Valerie wrapped her cool arms around him, her fingers tangling in his hair, he could not fight back. He had held out shakily, like a tree that had been hacked down to its breaking point. But that kiss was the last swing, the final impact, and he gave in finally, felled.

His fingers, roughened by work, stroked her cheek as they breathed together.

"I've been hungry for you for so long." He inhaled, combing fingers through her long corn-silk hair.

But just then, Valerie felt that same gaze she'd felt at the festival, those grape eyes, the weight of being watched. She heard something move at the mouth of the alley. This time, it was not a boar's head.

"Peter, did you hear that?"

He didn't even bother answering. He moved his warm hands to lift her, to carry her into the nearby granary and up the stairs, and then to press her against the roughness of the wall, and Valerie forgot everything else.

"Better?" he managed to get out.

Valerie couldn't reply. She felt every inch of his body pushing against hers as he lightly ran his hands over her waist. His hands searched for the laces on her bodice. Finding them, he tugged until they loosened.

Peter's face wasn't smooth; his hands weren't soft.

"Peter..." Her hand roamed, then rested high on his thigh. She was there and he was there, and his body was pressing up hard against her. She wanted to stamp her body upon his forever, to feel the imprint. His clothes, hers, everything that was between them, felt suddenly unbearable, and she longed to touch him, to really touch him, with her hands and her being and her everything.

Peter lowered her onto the straw lining the granary loft. Valerie looked up at the tall, shadowy interior of the dome. It was dizzying, like being inside the paneled chambers of an oak kaleidoscope.

His breath was ragged and uneven against her neck. The heat reverberated through her body like a flood let loose. Valerie had to remind herself to breathe.

He was opening her blouse, which had come untucked from her skirt. Rough fingers traversed her skin as his hands made their way inside. It was too much, she realized. She gasped, thinking she had to get away, unprepared for the intensity of his desire, when a clatter sounded from down below.

They pulled apart.

"Quick," Peter said, pulling her up and ushering her behind a post, so that only he was visible to the intruder.

"Peter!" someone called. He peered down. Two wood-cutters were loading a keg into a wheelbarrow.

"Peter, give us a hand, would you?"

Peter cast Valerie a desperate look. She beckoned him over a moment. Peter leaned over and pretended to shake a pebble from his boot as Valerie whispered, "The only life I want is with you," before pulling him to her and giving him charged, fiery kisses, one after the other. Peter reeled, touched her burning cheek, and took off.

Leaning against the post, Valerie still sensed the hot, lingering trace of his skin on hers. It had been overwhelming, and yet she wanted to hold the moment safe forever.

Valerie felt the sensation again that she was being watched. Instinctively, she looked up. A beady-eyed crow perched at the top of the tower cast down its searching black look, unfolded its wings, and took flight.

From behind his post, Henry Lazar saw Valerie sense his presence and look up. Shame pooled inside him like something wet. His feelings were cut off, snipped, like a length of ribbon. Watching her and Peter, he had tried to leave but couldn't look away. Instead, he stood frozen, horrified, transfixed by the intensity of the wretched, beautiful sight.

He stood a moment more, tensed the muscles in his jaw, and crept away.

Valerie waited until the men's voices had died down, become faint, and disappeared. Only then did she put her weight back on her feet and steal out the side door to return to the celebration, glad to get away.

She saw no sign of Peter. A line of figures was backlit by the tall pink flames, pulsing to the throb of the music. It seemed no one had noticed her absence. Even Roxanne was busy, watching in awe as fire walkers spun around, doing backflips, walking on their palms across the coals, kicking their feet high in the air. Everything was suddenly so beautiful.

Charged with an animal's ferocity, Valerie felt she could do anything. The tavern owner lumbered by wearing a pair of goat horns tied under his chin. Pulling her hair out of her face, she quickly wound it into a loose braid, her hands working instinctively. Then she grabbed the horns right off his head and strapped them onto her own.

Metal goblets were strewn atop the stacked bales of hay, ale seeping slowly through the tightly packed bundles and trickling out the bottom. Hearing laughter overhead, Valerie looked up. A few men were sitting in a tree and sloshing their drinks between parted boughs onto those people walking by underneath. One of the victims considered being angry but decided to laugh instead. Someone keeled into the bushes, and a brave soul went in after him. Some farmers hacked drunkenly at branches, and every now and then a big one came crashing down. People heard it, but in the night's clamor, they didn't even bother to look.

Suddenly, the smoldering coals of the bonfire stood for everything Valerie had been through, for the losses, the failures, the regrets. The music pounded as she ran past Roxanne and over to the red embers on the ground. As she danced across them, she was weightless, existing only as movement. The feeling was over just as soon as Valerie realized it had begun, and she ran off the coals onto the ground and looked behind her, at where she had just been.

Roxanne, having followed, was hurtling toward her, shrieking with laughter. Then they were in each other's arms, spinning, spinning. Valerie couldn't see anything, her revolving view of the world condensed into a blur. What was out there was not real. What had been real was the feel of Peter's hands, the weight of his body, the touch of his breath.

But one thing broke away from the others. A pair of girls who had been inspired to follow them over the coals were a dizzy mass of color. Their bodies danced past, revealing something in the alley that cut through the blur and arrested Valerie's attention.

"Where have you been anyway?" Roxanne asked, oblivious, gulping down air.

A pair of eyes.

Valerie stopped short, jostling Roxanne.

"What's the matter with you? You know, I was looking for you."

They did not speak for a moment, allowing the world to stop spinning. Roxanne was holding out expectantly for a response. But Valerie was elsewhere, far away in time.

She was seven years old, a little girl in the black forest, held in terror, pinned by a pair of savage eyes.

Eyes that *saw* her.

Not an ordinary kind of seeing, but seeing in a way that no one had seen her before. Seeing through her. Recognizing her.

The Wolf.

She had always known this day would come. As she had walked through the ordinariness of her everyday life, she had known it, but she'd never allowed herself to think it. But she had known.

And here it was.

First there came a low growl, unheard amidst the tumult of the festivities. But it was like a drop of water that starts a tidal wave.

With a roar and one ranging leap, the Wolf was already past Valerie and in the center of the town square.

The Reeve, holding forth at the table of honor, squinted at the monstrous dark shape before him, his face knotting up in an attempt at understanding. His alcohol-flooded mind struggled for recognition. He'd seen a shape like it only yesterday, in the cave, but this couldn't be a wolf; the beast that had turned him into a hero was a mere lapdog compared to this...*thing*.

But the eyes—the burning yellow eyes...its gargantuan blackness...its fur sculpted by the muscle underneath...
Horrible.

The Reeve rose to his feet unsteadily, his hand fumbling for the knife at his belt, knowing everyone was watching.

The great black shadow streaked toward him, quick as an arrow, and an instant later it had passed him. But an instant was enough. The Reeve stood motionless as a dark line widened on his throat, and then he dropped to the ground. One moment he'd been grinning, holding court in all his glory; the next, he was dead.

"We're under attack!" someone thought to yell.

Panic tore through the village like scissors through fine silk as the Wolf prowled the square. Scrambling off the stage, villagers collapsed into the well. Bottles were tossed, buckets of apples kicked over, instruments abandoned and rocking on their sides, their strings still quivering. Men did not stop to help up women who'd fallen into the muddy slush, so the women climbed out on their own, dripping skirts clutched in hands that were too shocked even to tremble.

Claude had been standing by himself, shuffling his cards, still hoping William might come back with his hat. Catching the terror, Claude whirled in a panic, causing the cards to fly from his hands. They fell slowly, like petals, settling bright in the dirt. He dropped to his hands and knees, grappling for his scattered treasure. He had to get up, he knew, but he also knew that if he left even one card, that everything gone wrong would never be righted, and that wrongness would grow like a fungus until it engulfed the whole world.

As he crawled to reach under a wagon for The Falling Tower card, he froze. On the other side of the wagon, a man was going by on his back, his head and limbs bumping along like a sack of apples against the ground as the Wolf dragged him through the snow. Once they had passed, Claude could see what they had been blocking; it was one of the village seamstresses who only two months before had won the embroidery contest for an image of The Lover Returning from a Hunt, which her nimble needle had recreated on a lady's pocket handkerchief. Now she was pitifully slumped against the earth, her life's blood spurting from her in a hot, black rush.

And it came over him, there on all fours like a dog, that he could never stem the flooding darkness; his life was infinitesimally small, and no matter what he did, the bright card deck of life would always be scattered and ground into the dirt of this suffering world. Claude crouched, his body racked with a sob.

Valerie stood amidst the madness, in a place beyond fear.

Why is everyone running? What has life ever given them? All along, they've belonged to the Wolf. And now he's returned to collect what was always his.

But then four villagers came striding past her, hidden in their cloaks, strangely unafraid.

The reason came as they threw off their disguises and drew weapons — a wickedly glimmering silver sword, a pair of murderous battle axes, and bullwhips as heavy as steel cables. They were Father Solomon's soldiers. They had simply been waiting in the wings for the real show to begin.

One of them, the Captain, gave Valerie a hard-bitten smile.

"Run and hide, girl," he whispered.

They strode into the carnage, and from the other corners of the square, the rest of Father Solomon's men closed in.

Valerie looked around, tracking the creature.

The Wolf had its claws planted in the back of the village butcher, but its ears pricked up at the sound of a ferocious battle cry, and it looked around, a still-writhing arm clenched in its massive jaws. It saw a pair of battle axes descending, one whirling in each hand of a huge Viking of a man. The Wolf appeared paralyzed by the storm of metal, but as the axes came down to deliver double death, there was a snarling blur of motion, too fast for any eye to see, and the awesome battle cry twisted into a horrible shriek. The axes flew into the air, one cleaving into the snowy earth, the other meeting the face of an unfortunate fleeing villager, his blood spattering.

With one great lunge, the Wolf was instantly twenty yards away, pursuing another of Solomon's men, leaving the Viking fallen atop the one-armed body of the butcher.

Floating through the nightmare, Valerie came upon an impossible sight: the scribe, diligently drawing the chaos, standing close enough to see details. His hand moved quickly, his eyes quicker, seeing the beast in fragments: haunches, fur, teeth, tongue. He did not look at his parchment. He spared a second to look at Valerie, gave her a sad smile that suggested the artist was horrified by what he saw but was driven by some perverse human need to record it.

Valerie watched him edge closer to the Wolf, close enough to see the electricity pricking up the fur of its back, the slobber dripping from its jaw. His quill scratched at the page, brown ink dappling the papyrus sheet. He shook the quill to loosen the ink, and that little motion was just enough to turn the Wolf's eyes upon him. Valerie finally covered her mouth in horror as she watched the scribe hold up the quill—was it in self-defense? Or was it to say, *Look, I'm only an artist?*

No matter. It was the last gesture of his life.

Valerie went to his body and retrieved his final work from the ground so that it would not be rubbed out in blood and filth. A mighty stallion brushed past her, neighing as the wind whipped its mane into its eyes. Father Solomon sat astride it, shouting.

"Get to the church!" he cried out over the panic. "The Wolf cannot cross onto holy ground!" As he drew his sword and rode over the body of the Reeve, Valerie felt that he savored the vindication. He had warned them, they had chosen not to listen, and now they had paid the price. It felt good to be right, Valerie knew, even about things one would prefer to be wrong about. "Your time has come, beast!"

Silver armor glittered in the firelight as the hunter rode toward the fray. Valerie wondered if Solomon's sword would get lost in the Wolf's matted, thick fur. Was any weapon big enough to fell such a creature?

The towering Wolf effigy had become an orange smear against the sky.

Solomon's men sailed toward the Wolf, keeping low to the ground. No fear or rage registered on the beast's face. Rather, Valerie imagined it was a look of mild annoyance. Almost amusement.

One soldier approached the Wolf, swinging a chain with

a spiked ball at either end. The weapon appeared violent by its simplicity. And just as simply, the Wolf took him down.

Another swarthy soldier rushed forward next with a curved saber, harsh and beautiful in his rage. He seemed stunned as the Wolf's claws found their mark, and his skin popped as it was punctured, letting loose a long spray of blood from the slit between his upper and lower breastplates.

And still the soldiers attacked, one after another, giving the Wolf no rest.

Finally, the Captain came running, snapping his bull-whip out as an expression of his ferocity. His body was tight and neat; he looked more like a beautiful sculpture than a person. Strutting forward, his brother came up alongside him, pulling out his own bullwhip, which was wound into a tight coil. He unleashed it in preparation.

The two men flanked the Wolf. A third soldier stood behind them, breathing hard, his lance at the ready. The two men moved like dolphins, arcing and flipping as they lashed the ropes. Most of the villagers had heeded Solomon's warning by now and fled to the church. But Valerie stood, watching, feeling her insides stretched as taut as the leather whips.

They thought they'd caught it.

But, ensnared, the Wolf planted its legs and started backing up, tugging the soldiers by their two strained leashes.

The huge men slid forward in the dirt, trying to maintain their balance, careful not to lean too far forward or back. Their legs quivered as they struggled with the beast. Their combined weight was, to the Wolf, not much of a burden.

Then something broke, some inevitable release of tension, and Valerie felt her heart fall like a stone as the Captain was dragged to one side through the blood-tracked snow and the Wolf hurled his brother across the square, his flat body flashing through the air like a star.

The Captain's brother struggled to get up, but the Wolf ripped him back down to earth.

Valerie looked up at Father Solomon astride his mighty steed, and in his face, she saw what she would never have imagined.

Uncertainty.

The man who had come prepared for everything had been caught by surprise.

The soldier with the lance turned and strode toward Solomon, who had kept a hard, eagle eye on the scene.

"It's strong—stronger than any we've faced before!"

"Have faith. God is stronger," Solomon said, staring straight ahead and spurring his steed, the handle of his blade nestled tightly against his hand.

Across the square, the Wolf reacted to the name of the divinity. It whirled to face Father Solomon, letting out a low growl. Solomon met the monster's eyes. He reached down, and, taking the crucifix that hung by a chain from his neck, he kissed it.

Valerie saw whatever it was that had overtaken him—

doubt, fear—had now left him, and the man of certainty returned with a vengeance.

"God is stronger!"

And with that, he snapped the reins and dug his spurs into the sides of his steed. As the horse charged, Solomon raised his sword—the sword of God's wrath.

But the Wolf held its ground. Fearless. Challenging.

And its jaws spread, letting forth an unearthly roar that shook the ground where Valerie stood.

Solomon's horse spooked, rearing up, crossing its feet over one another, tripping over its own legs, sending its rider flying backward into the air. He came slamming to earth amidst the blazing coals of the bonfire, throwing up a geyser of sparks. The horse's hooves drummed the ground as it galloped away.

Solomon's scream of agony and rage seemed to amuse the Wolf. Valerie could feel the pleasure in every ripple of its muscles as it charged toward the coals to finish off its helpless enemy. Struggling to get out of the fire, his sword lost, Solomon knew his end had come.

Zzzzziiiissssss! Slanting shadows came jetting across the square from nowhere.

No, not from nowhere—the masked bowman seated on the rail of the tavern balcony wielded a fire crossbow that spat out silver-tipped arrows repeatedly. The bolts zippered toward the Wolf, who let out a snarl of outrage and, with a mighty leap, soared onto the top of a cottage. The bowman sent bolt upon bolt after the shadow bounding across the rooftops.

With a final spring, the beast vanished into the night.

But the show wasn't over. Valerie watched a figure climb out of the burning coals and smoke, brushing hot cinders from his face. He was burned, scarred for life. But spurred by pain and hatred, by bitter anger and a thirst for vengeance, Father Solomon rose.

Resurrected.

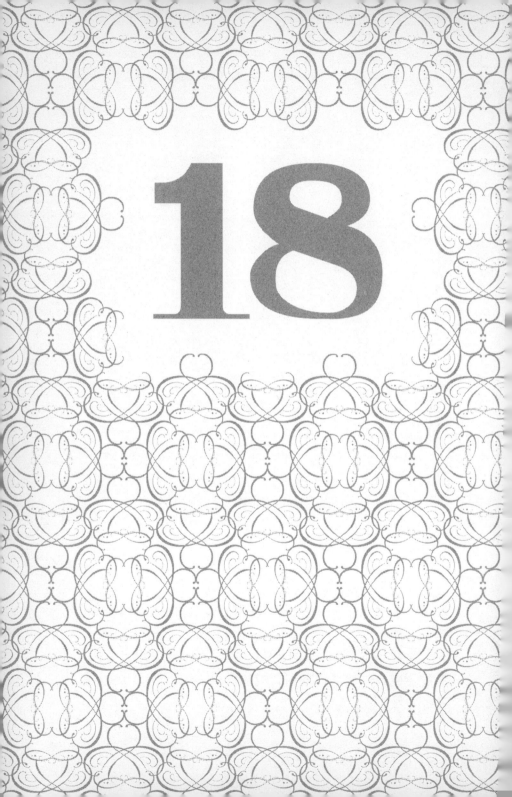

18

It was tracking two shapes. *Human shapes. Vulnerable.*

"Claude," one of them whimpered, barely able to get out the word.

Pathetic. But a pathetic whimper rings loud in the ears of a predator.

That and the pounding of a human girl's heart.

Moving through the wreckage, her eyes burning from the smoke, Valerie felt isolated, separate from the events she had just witnessed, as if she were behind a wall of glass. She vaguely wondered why she was not among the dead. Why had she been spared when her own sister had not?

And why wasn't she terrified to the bone like Roxanne, shaking at her side?

"Claude!" Roxanne called again, her voice panicky. "Where are you?"

Roxanne knew better than to trust her mother to worry about Claude. But she and Valerie hadn't found her brother among the cowering townfolk, packed tightly like guppies in the church. They had found their parents, and lost them just as quickly, as they continued on.

And so far, they hadn't found Claude among the dead.

So far.

Nor had Valerie found Peter. She wanted to call out for him, too, but Daggorhorn was a town that fed on scandal. So, even in the midst of tragedy, she guarded her secret.

There was something else that kept her from calling. A suspicion that had started to rise up inside her that so far, her mind had only flirted with, refusing to embrace it. *All this had started when Peter arrived....It had to be a coincidence....*

She sensed movement close by and looked around carefully, not wanting to alarm Roxanne. But even that was enough.

"*What?* Is there something?"

"No. It's nothing."

She laid a reassuring hand on her friend's arm as she considered their next move.

"This way," she said, guiding Roxanne into Dye Makers Alley.

As the Wolf followed the figures around the corner, the pungent scent of dye ripped through the scent of the one girl's fear.

But what of the other girl?

How strange it is to stalk one who doesn't reek of terror.

Valerie was thinking of Lucie. This was a place that they had always loved, a narrow magical pathway with a carpet of petals fallen around the dye vats like flakes dropped from a twilight sky. Valerie had grown up coming there, always desperate to slip her dusty feet into or skim her hands along the inviting surface of the yawning blue water. She had done it once. But Lucie, the big girl, had caught her, pulling her blueberry palm out of the long, low vat. To make amends, Lucie had stolen a handful of flowers from the storage towers and carefully woven them that night into Valerie's hair.

If only flowers lived forever.

If only sisters did, too.

Something startled Roxanne, who let out a shriek, lurching forward. Valerie grabbed her wrist, pulling her back from the lip of a vat of blue dye, shimmering garnet in the moonlight.

"Careful!"

A clatter echoed behind them. They whirled. Valerie's heart hung in her chest as if suspended in the moment just before free fall.

The Wolf was coming through the smoke. Ravenous, snarling, showing its dagger teeth caked with blood.

Valerie spun back around, yanking the frozen Roxanne along with her. They ran, their feet throwing up a spray of petals in their wake.

But the alley reached a dead end. Nowhere to go. Valerie cursed herself for not thinking of this. There was only the wall of storage towers full of cut flowers for the dye. A ladder of spikes was driven into the wood. Valerie jumped, grabbing hold of one and pulling herself up. She looked down. The Wolf was nowhere in sight. Maybe it had lost interest.

But Roxanne was frozen. Valerie reached down.

"Grab my hand!"

"I can't."

"Do it!"

But Roxanne didn't move. Valerie let go of the spike, landed by Roxanne, ready to shake her out of her paralysis— but then the Wolf sprang down in front of Valerie.

It was colossal, so big that it was everywhere, taller than any man who had ever walked the earth. This was the evil thing that had buried its teeth in her sister's flesh. Valerie felt her courage shrivel into panic.

But she could not take her eyes from the blazing gold of the Wolf's eyes.

The Wolf did not blink as they breathed in unison.

The world went quiet. Then Valerie heard an intricate voice, a medley woven from sounds both male and female, human and animal. A composite of every voice she'd ever known, it vibrated deep within her. The Devil's voice.

"Did you think you could outrun me?"

Valerie felt the sky whirl, the earth give way. "What—?" she responded. "You speak?"

"All that matters is that you understand me, Valerie."

Valerie smelled the thick sweetness of the flowers mixed with the gnarled musk of the Wolf.

"You know my name," she stated dumbly.

"What are you doing?" Roxanne asked Valerie, her voice tremulous.

The Wolf whirled on Roxanne, growling until her legs gave way, and she crumpled to a silent heap in the dirt. The Wolf, uninterested in Roxanne's fate, turned its eyes back upon Valerie. The demon voice came again, filling her mind, her body.

"We are alike, you and I."

"No." Valerie was quick, her very soul rejecting the idea. "No. You're a murderer. A monster. I'm *nothing* like you."

She reached behind her, groping blindly for something to grab hold of. There was nothing.

"You've killed, too. I know your secrets."

Valerie felt her breath rush back into her body, mixing with her heartbeat hammering in her chest. What the Wolf said had landed in a place deeper than hearing.

"You're a hunter," the Wolf continued, taunting her. **"I can smell it on you even now."**

Valerie couldn't help but wonder what the Wolf had said to Lucie. Her thoughts exploded all at once, paralyzing her.

The Wolf came closer. Valerie studied those gorgeous yellow eyes.

"What...big...eyes...you...have...." she said faintly.

"The better to see you with, my dear."

Mesmerized by the intensity of that incredible stare, Valerie couldn't look away from the horror of what happened next. The skin on either side of the Wolf's brow separated, slit open in an ungodly blossoming to reveal...*a second pair of eyes*.

A pair of eyes more striking than the first. Sensitive and intelligent. All-knowing.

Human.

Before Valerie could react, the Wolf spoke again, its massive tail swishing the dust from side to side.

"I see what lies in your heart," it said. Its wet charcoal lips were so black that they were purple, and its craggy teeth were spaced in uneven rows, with only darkness where some were missing or misaligned.

"You want to escape from Daggorhorn. You want freedom."

For a moment, Valerie thought like a wolf. She found that she could.

She felt what it would be like to run free, to race through a dark forest, blood awakened, to close in on the kill. To live a life unfettered by fear, by ties or bonds. To do whatever she wanted, unburdened by place, freed from living the life of an insect, shuttling back and forth within the same minuscule radius. She felt the vision of this new life overwhelming her, severing her connection to the present.

"No..." she tried to say.

But the Wolf, those eyes, saw that it had touched something, a truth.

"Come away with me," it said. Valerie hesitated, and the Wolf filled the gap of silence. **"Come away with me,"** it repeated.

I've heard that before.

Somewhere in the distance, there were shouts, the clamor of soldiers, the clanking of armor. The noise helped clear her head.

"Father Solomon will stop you." Valerie heard how she sounded. Like a little girl, helpless, alone, covering her face, waiting for someone else to appear to make everything better.

The Wolf straightened to its full height, drawing its shoulder blades back. Its shadow fell over both girls' faces.

"Father Solomon doesn't know what he's dealing with."

The Wolf had taken on a new tone. **"Come away with me or I will kill everyone you love."**

Valerie shook with the weight of what she was being asked to do; how could she choose?

The Wolf's ears flicked back in impatience. **"Starting with your friend here."**

It made a lunge for Roxanne, snapping its colossal jaw.

Impossibly, at that exact moment, two figures appeared out of the shadows. The masked bowman was already opening fire on the Wolf even as he and Solomon rounded the corner into the alley.

"I'll return for you." The Wolf bent to Valerie. **"Before the blood moon wanes."**

As the Wolf heaved itself over the wall, Solomon snatched the crossbow and fired off a flurry of arrows, but the Wolf was already disappearing into the night.

Solomon clambered up after it but could not make it over the top of the wall. He shot and rearmed, shot and rearmed, not taking his eyes off the Wolf as it loped into the distance.

Quivering with the strain of holding in his rage and power, Solomon jumped catlike back to the ground. Valerie saw that his cheek was black and red and yellow, like different candles melted together. He reached down to feel the dye in the vats, bringing a scoop to his face, smelling it. He let the handful drop and flicked the water off his palms.

He began to lead the girls to the churchyard, but as they passed through the square, where the fire was only embers now, he was intercepted by a panic-stricken woman. "God save us!"

"God will save only those who have earned his love through *faith and action*," he said, looking past them in the direction the Wolf had gone. He reminded Valerie of a hornet, a quick-eyed commander buzzing with wounded vanity.

Valerie remembered Roxanne and looked over at her. She was gnawing on her thumb. All color had left her face, making her freckles stand out like speckles dotting a robin's egg.

The Captain was speaking in another language to a soldier at the church gate, his voice dipping into lower tones. He paused to usher them into the churchyard. The image on the gate of Christ as a wolf slayer, thrusting a dagger through a wolf's chest, gave Valerie shivers.

"Here you will be assured of your safety." The Captain switched tongues, sliding easily into English.

"But my brother! I have to find him," Roxanne protested.

"If he is alive, you'll find him inside."

"Wait!" she shouted, but he'd already slammed shut the heavy iron gate behind them.

Valerie looked at her friend with pity. She was still worried about where Peter had gone, too.

"I'm sure he's safe, Roxanne. He has his own ways."

Roxanne stared back at her as though she were a stranger.

"You talked to the Wolf," Roxanne whispered accusingly, her thin voice cut with fear.

"I had to. It talked to us." Valerie thought she was agreeing with her.

"No," Roxanne corrected. "It *growled* at us...." The fear in her eyes took on new depths. "You heard it *talk* to you?"

Valerie realized then the enormity of what had just occurred. Roxanne hadn't heard a word. It was only *her*. In a town like this, the hazard of anyone knowing she possessed such a skill was monumental. She glanced around to see if anyone was listening.

Valerie thought of the rumors that would proliferate if anyone knew. And then she turned those same glares and whispers upon herself. Why *had* the Wolf spoken to her? Why hadn't Roxanne also understood? Valerie felt claustrophobic in her own skin.

"They'll call me a witch. Don't tell anyone," she begged, her voice raw.

Roxanne gave her a look. She seemed to accept Valerie's fear as an acknowledgment of her own.

"Of course not. Obviously."

Valerie felt grateful that Roxanne was not the kind of girl who would think to ask what the Wolf had said.

She snuck a look at her friend, who was stalking forward to the church door, her colorless face staring willfully ahead. She looked exactly the way a girl who had been hunted by a werewolf *should* look. Valerie again wondered why she herself wasn't more traumatized. It all seemed... like nature's way, as if this were the order of things.

224

Looking at Roxanne, Valerie saw a drop of blood fall, and then another.

Roxanne reached for her face and felt wetness beneath her nose. After all the slaughter she had seen, it was only a simple nosebleed.

Roxanne shook her head and walked into the church. Valerie watched her friend, and then she tilted her face up to the sky. A revelation struck Valerie as she stood alone looking up at the spire of the church. Those eyes, the second pair of eyes the Wolf had revealed to her.

They had been familiar.

Part Three

19

Waking at dawn, Valerie could taste the bitter cold on her tongue like rust. She looked around, embarrassed. She had been dreaming of Peter, of his touch. And yet, the image went sour when she remembered the carnage.

Where is he?

Valerie fought back the thought and stood up from the hard church pew to stretch her back. The door to the refuge was wide open. She could see that Daggorhorn was draped in a fog, a gauze curtain through which the village looked pale and desolate.

The Captain had opened the churchyard gates. She passed through them and saw a few men at work gathering the charred and bloody remains that littered the square.

All was quiet but for the scraping of shovels against winter ground. The mist wound its way around a maze of trees. The air felt too close, and the people were antsy.

She saw Henry passing through the square, but he did not seem to see her. Maybe he was embarrassed about how he had acted at the festival. She almost called out to him but stopped herself, thinking of what had followed, of Peter's hands on her. Little did Henry know that she was the one who should have been feeling shamed.

She heard the clatter of hooves as Solomon's horse came into view. With its legs cloaked in the low-lying fog, it looked like it was floating. Its rider, his face blackened and bloody, came to a halt and surveyed the carnage. He wore long black robes with embroidery on the shoulders. Holding one glove between his teeth, he deliberately pulled off the other. Valerie was stunned to see that his fingernails were plated with silver and sharpened into daggers. They gleamed dully, matte and clean, his cuticles pushed back neatly to meet the nail bed.

Clutching his robes in his hands, Father Auguste bustled to catch up with the older man. Father Solomon looked down at him, not bothering to mask his scorn.

"I am sorry," Auguste said in a clammy voice. "We never should have doubted you. We will never make that mistake again."

Those gathered waited for Father Solomon's reaction. *From now on*, the villagers silently decided, *we will place our hopes on him.*

He dismounted his horse and walked slowly, with purpose, knowing the eyes of the village were on him.

"I've never seen a beast as strong as this. The curse is hereditary, and each generation is more potent than the one before, but I've never seen one from such a long bloodline. I don't just want to kill this beast."

Not kill the beast?

"Not anymore. I want to make it suffer."

He came to the Reeve's fallen body, lying beside the overturned banquet table. "I hope he enjoyed his celebration," Solomon said, lightly kicking the snow beside the wounded man. The body looked so lifeless lying among the rest of the wreckage that no one even flinched. Everyone felt certain that the Reeve had not felt it, that whatever he might have been had long departed and nothing of him remained there on that barren, frost-hardened ground.

Solomon noticed the Captain, bent over his brother's body, clutching a leg as though it were a baby. Poisoned tendrils radiated from the wound. The body looked like it had been packed full, like the muscles were straining beneath his skin.

Solomon strode over. "A man bitten," he said to the Captain, expressionless as marble, "is a man cursed."

Valerie watched in shock as Solomon drew his sword and plunged it into the man's chest. The Captain closed his eyes, and when he opened them, they had hardened. He released his brother's limb and turned away.

Solomon turned, unaffected, to address the crowd.

"Villagers of Daggorhorn," he said, his voice unbroken. "Now it is time to be serious."

The villagers liked his authoritative tone; they wanted to be given a plan. They were impressed with the action he had just taken: The Captain's brother had been an outsider, and in death, he had become a threat to their safety. He had been taken care of swiftly, unsentimentally.

"There will be no more celebrating"—Solomon bent down to retrieve a pig mask abandoned in the snow— "until the werewolf is found in its human form. And destroyed. By whatever means necessary."

Solomon let the mask drop. His men gathered around him. This time, they did not conceal their weapons.

"It could be any of you. Which is why we will look everywhere. The signs will be subtle: isolation, witchcraft, black arts, strange scents.... Your homes will be searched. Your secrets will be brought to light. If you're innocent, you have nothing to fear. But if you're guilty, I swear on my children that you will be destroyed."

Solomon saw the villagers noticing his soldiers, their weapons.

"My wife died. Your fathers, your sons, your daughters have died. Let some of us remain alive to remember them," he said, stepping through the strewn detritus of the previous night.

There were murmurs, emphatic nods throughout the crowd, as the villagers looked at their neighbors, friends, husbands and wives, children. Valerie felt a strange need to speak up but couldn't bring herself to. She felt uneasy, seeing how eager her neighbors were to obey this new authority.

Her stomach creaked like a door, and Valerie realized she'd forgotten about eating. She ducked behind the crowd and headed for home, glad for a reason not to listen.

Valerie's father and grandmother were there, but all she saw was her mother. Suzette looked small and thin, her skin hanging loose like it didn't fit, as though she'd purchased a face that was a size too large. Her chest and neck were covered in a thin sheen of sweat, her wavy hair matted to her skull. Lying on the bed, she was dwarfed by a quilt that Grandmother's mother had made.

Suzette's face had been slashed by the Wolf.

The blood had dried in a thick clump over her cheek like a crust of bread, and it was impossible to see how much damage had been done.

Cesaire looked up as Valerie entered. He pulled her to him. Then Grandmother took Valerie's hand while Cesaire tended to the water boiling in the fireplace.

Watching her father, Valerie drifted into thoughts of another time.

We used to know a bath was coming when we saw the four pots of water set over the fire. My mother would come in, pulling her dress over her head, disheveling her hair. Her body was beautiful, I knew even as a girl. It glowed like there was something magical underneath her skin. She would put the two of us into the trough first, lifting us under our armpits and resting us gently in the warm water. And then she'd ease herself in slowly, her legs slipping around us, careful as they hugged our sides, my sister next to her, and then me. I always felt like I was on the outside with Lucie and my mother.

We girls took turns leaning back to dunk our heads underneath. When it was my turn, I would swish my hair around from side to side, back and forth, back and forth, so that I felt like a mermaid.

That time was gone now. Valerie was afraid her mind would shed her sister's image, a coping mechanism that Valerie didn't want to kick in. Memory was always decaying. She had so many memories that she wished she could stop creating new ones, because there was already so much experience to make sense of, and yet with every moment she was making more.

She looked now at what remained.

Her father was caring for his wife, bringing warm, wet rags to dab at her face. Was this tenderness? Valerie wondered. A performance for Grandmother? Or had Lucie been right? Was this love?

Valerie saw Cesaire's eyes resting upon Suzette's reclining form. Valerie wondered whether he really saw her there anymore. After eighteen years of marriage, Cesaire did not seem to notice her gentleness with their children or her sun-streaked hair in the summer months. Was that what marriage was, an inability to see who the person was, the way that we don't know ourselves because we stand too close? Was that what she would have with Henry? With Peter?

Valerie knew her parents had been present for the same traumas and tragedies, and yet, they had not experienced them together. They'd gone through them separately, at the same time.

Suzette, perhaps sensing this appraisal, swung her hand, sending a tin basin on the bed stand clattering to the floor. As Valerie bent down for it, her mother continued to moan.

Remembering Solomon's story, Valerie went over the details of the night before: Had she seen the Wolf get slashed? Where had her mother been?

Is my mother the Wolf? Valerie could not stand to think about it, and so when Grandmother nudged her toward her mother, Valerie went without hesitation.

There was the sound of heavy boots mounting the ladder, then pounding on the door. So they had come, just as they'd said they would, to tear apart their homes, to strip them bare. The inquisitors would pry open their lives, dig out their secrets.

What do we have to hide? Valerie asked herself.

Bang! Bang! Bang! The pounding became more insistent.

Valerie kept the chain lock bolted as she cracked open the door, expecting to greet the Captain or Solomon himself.

Instead she met a pair of eyes that were burning, urgent... frightening. Like those she had seen in a dark alley.

"Peter?"

"Valerie, open the door."

Valerie hesitated; something in her felt she shouldn't. He pushed on it, and it cracked under the pressure, but the chain held.

"*Open* it."

Why was he being so savage?

"You shouldn't be here," she heard her voice say.

"We're all in danger," Peter hissed. "We've got to leave."

Through the crack in the door, his pupils were needle thin, glowing like they'd been heated in a fire. She thought of the boy he'd been and finally acknowledged he was not that boy anymore.

"Get your things. Quick. Come away with me."

Valerie thought of the granary, of his breath on her body, how it had felt like he wanted to devour her.

Come away with me or I will kill everyone you love.

He hadn't said that—had he? No, that was the Wolf.

But here were his blazing, dangerous eyes, staring in at her. Pushing on the door. Pulling on her heart. Trying to lure her away.

She stepped back the way she'd step back from a wagon hurtling by at full speed.

"Valerie, there's no time."

It had been only two days, but so much had changed since she was ready to go away with him, since she'd trusted him enough for that. Since then, her sister had been murdered. Her town had been ravaged. Her mother, attacked.

Since the Wolf had come.... *Since Peter had come.*

"Hurry, Valerie."

She shook her mind clear, forced herself to say something, anything.

"I can't. My mother's been hurt."

"How come I didn't kill it when I had the chance?" Peter growled, stepping back to throw a rock into the street below, hard, as though it contained all of his regrets.

And in that instant, while his hands were off the door, she darted forward, pushed it shut. Slid the bolt into place.

His voice came back to the door. "What are you doing?"

"I don't have a choice. I'm sorry."

She leaned on the door, waiting to hear the sound of him leaving. Doubt sifted through her like the coldest, finest grains of sand. Had she made the right choice? Or had fear turned her against the person she loved the most?

When she heard his footsteps withdrawing, she peered through the leaded panes of the window. She caught sight of something in his back pocket.

A knife.

Peter had stolen a knife. We were seven years old, and we'd caught a rabbit in a trap. We looked at each other darkly, a look I'll never forget, one of a shared savage thrill, like young wolves taking down their first kill....

A spill of blood issued from the rabbit's neck, a quick red streak across pristine white fur, slow enough to be cruel. I hadn't cut deep enough. Had I wanted to spare its life or prolong its misery? I've never wanted to know the answer.

Was it Peter or I who pushed the other into killing?
The Wolf knew I had killed before.
The Wolf.
Peter.
Can it be?
Her fears were confirmed. And yet...

As the wind howled down the chimney, Valerie saw Grandmother leaning over a still-moaning Suzette, changing her bandages. The wavering firelight distorted the old lady's shadow, changing it into something grotesque and monstrous dancing upon the wall. Valerie crept forward and gaped at the horrible claw marks on her mother's face, then at Grandmother's fingernails. Why hadn't she ever noticed how long those nails were... how like *claws* they were?

Valerie's hand reached out to take hold of an elk-horn knife on the nightstand, slipping it into her cuff.

Something clamped onto her leg like a shackle, stopping her breath. But it was only her poor mother remembering the moment the Wolf chiseled out her flesh with its razor-sharp claws.

"Don't leave me alone," Suzette's voice rattled.

Cesaire had washed her face clean of the blood until it was striped pink and white, ridged like a seashell. Her fragile beauty had been taken from her. She was disfigured.

Another eighth of an inch and it would have gotten her eye. Was the Wolf precise or inexact?

Valerie's frail, ruined mother lifted her cup of sleeping

tea to her mouth with both hands. Grandmother helped her take a sip. Valerie watched her carefully. Odd how she'd never realized before that Grandmother's sleeping teas were really just weak poisons. Poisons that left one helpless.

Suzette's eyelids flickered, then fell shut.

"Rest, dear," Grandmother instructed her, her voice like a lullaby as she motioned Valerie away from the bed.

No one had been caring for the cottage since Lucie's death, and a half-dozen plums were rotting in a bowl. Empty mugs and crumby plates cluttered the sink.

Grandmother handed Valerie a crust of bread and then bustled around cleaning up. Grandmother was more attuned to Valerie, to her needs and wants, than she herself was. The bread was just out of the oven, and all she could taste was the heat. She ate it anyway, mindlessly. *Bite, chew, swallow.*

"Something's wrong. What is it, darling? Do you want to tell me?"

Her grandmother was trying to find out information, to pry her open like a stubborn walnut shell, to know her inside and out. *She wants to know everything. Why?* She already knew all of Valerie's secrets.

Valerie looked at her grandmother. Her eyes. Dark brown. Burning. Compelling Valerie to answer.

"The Wolf. It talked to me."

Disbelief flickered across Grandmother's face. "And you understood it?" She leaned her body against the kitchen table, and behind her back, her hand searched secretly for something....

"Just as clearly as I understand you." Valerie heard a catch in her own voice, a challenge.

Grandmother's hand found what it was groping for—*a pair of scissors.*

And Valerie's hand clenched something inside her cuff— *the elk-horn knife.*

They stood facing each other, the poisoned silence winding its way around them, choking them.

"Whom have you told about this?" Grandmother's lips twitched at the corner.

Their bodies were tense with what was unspoken between them.

"No one knows but Roxanne. She won't tell anyone. She won't even talk to me about it."

"The Wolf chose not to kill you...."

Hearing the timbre of her voice, Valerie suddenly felt sure. It wasn't her mother, it wasn't Peter. It was *her.* Valerie could feel it. The Wolf was there, in the room, in the body of her grandmother.

"...Because it certainly could have," Grandmother reminded her in an even tone.

"I think it wants me alive."

Valerie felt the air leave the room. Feeling smothered, she cautiously moved to open the shutters.

The purple morning poured into the room, mingled with a breeze carrying the familiar scent of pine, changing everything. Both women realized how wrong they had been. Grandmother's hand let go of the scissors behind her back, and she wiped the offending hand on the front of her apron, as though trying to wipe away her guilt. Valerie, too, felt ashamed of doubting this woman she had always loved. They both relaxed.

"But why you, Valerie?"

"I don't know. But it says if I don't go with it, it will kill everyone I love. It's already killed Lucie...."

Her neck hurt from the tension, and she made the decision to rest her head on Grandmother's shoulder. She let it hang there, feeling the weight of her head. Something cracked in her spine, fitting back into place.

Valerie felt Grandmother's hand reach for hers. Thinking about what she had been driven to, suspecting everyone around her, Valerie felt she had gone mad.

"It's coming for me," Valerie whispered. "Before the blood moon wanes."

Grandmother pulled away, deeply troubled. Looking for something to do, she decided on making tea. The handle of the kettle shook as her unsteady hands took it from the hearth.

"What happened to Lucie is my fault," Valerie stated. "The Wolf is here because of me."

Grandmother was silent, and Valerie understood that Grandmother could not deny it.

Valerie had to get out. She emerged from the cottage, amazed at the simple act of being able to walk away, like a hermit crab that had stepped out of its molted shell, feeling no pull, the weight of what it'd abandoned only a ghost of what once was. The chill hit her like a slap in the face, waking her from her stupor. Valerie walked quickly but aimlessly.

Picking her way to the well, she came across Roxanne and her mother retrieving water. Behind them, soldiers were ransacking a cottage, tossing aside the family's meager possessions.

"Has Claude come home?" she asked.

Roxanne moved past carrying a bucket in each hand. She acted as though she hadn't seen or heard Valerie.

"Nobody's seen him," Marguerite answered before moving on.

Valerie was stung. Roxanne knew that Valerie cared for Claude—she was the only other person who looked out for him when no one else would. Why had she brushed off Valerie's concern? Valerie scanned her memory as she peered into the blank depths of the well. Was it that Roxanne was ashamed of how fearful she'd acted in front of her?

Or was it because the Wolf had not chosen her? Valerie felt a wicked thrill from deep down inside herself. Maybe Roxanne was jealous. Maybe all the girls were jealous because of her betrothal.

The dog belonging to the visiting woodcutter ran up,

and Valerie bent down to pet it, holding out her hand. It was what she needed most in the world right then, for an innocent to come to her, to offer up its back for a stroke, to be trusted, told that she was good. But the dog looked at Valerie fearfully, refusing to come near her. Valerie stayed crouched, waiting, hoping, but the dog edged away, snapping its head back as it gave a few barks, and then turned and bounded off, tail between its legs. Like she was a threat.

Valerie was not who she had been. She felt parts of herself softly crumbling off, like a cliff falling into the sea.

She was still kneeling at the well, pulling at the old pump, when a dark shape passed over the water. Her stomach dipped.

It was Henry, different than she'd ever seen him. His eyes were dark and vacant, like empty rooms.

"I'm breaking off the engagement." His voice was ragged around the edges.

"Breaking it off?" Valerie didn't know how to feel.

"Yes," he said, blinking his eyes slowly as he said it, as though that might help the decision he'd made to sink in. "I saw you with Peter."

"Saw us?"

"In the granary."

The words seeped into her, soaking her through with awful understanding. She saw Henry's thoughts storming behind his eyes.

What a cruel joke to be played on him, she thought, waking up to the fullness of his feelings for her. To have loved a girl for so long, to have stood by without pressuring her, respecting her need for independence, and then to see that love shattered by *Peter* in an instant—by someone who swept in after being gone for years and then took what he wanted without a thought for her happiness.

She felt how much it must hurt to have his hope trampled on by the one Henry blamed for his most painful loss. *If only Lucie were here, if only he had loved* her *instead of me*.

"I'm not going to force you to marry me," Henry went on, not requiring her to respond, a gentleman to the end.

Somehow, her heart broke watching his do the same. Again, she thought of burying herself in his chest, of the safety he offered her. She'd had enough of danger, of trauma and passion. She was angry with herself; why couldn't she love Henry?

"I know you don't want to be with me."

His honesty was a shock.

Because it was all she could think to do, Valerie fumbled to unclasp her bracelet and, at last succeeding, gave it back to him.

"I'm so sorry." She heard herself saying the empty words,

something she'd tried never to do. Having nothing else, she used them anyway, knowing they were a pathetic offering.

He was gone in an instant, the only noise now the afternoon crawl of the muddy stream. Standing under the silent sun of mid-morning, she was left to weigh Henry's words. She couldn't think about it too long, though, because if she did, there came a shameful rush of fire, flames flicking and blazing behind her ribs.

Valerie had just shaken the snow from her red cloak and slipped it back on when she heard shouts from the direction of the granary. She followed the growing crowd there, relieved that the focus was on something besides herself.

The granary was a different place by day. Sunlight splintered between the slats, illuminating the cobwebs that lurked between beams and buttresses. Father Auguste was standing with Solomon and his soldiers, who had weapons at the ready. She followed his gaze upward . . . and she saw Claude.

He was alive. But perched on a rafter, cowering, shaking like he was covered with invisible insects or crabs, he seemed utterly traumatized. Or possessed. One of Solomon's archers raised his bow.

There was a scream as Roxanne came running and threw herself at the archer, only to be snatched back by the soldiers.

"*Ne conjugare nobiscum*," intoned the archer.

Valerie pushed her own way through the crowd and

stood beside Roxanne. "I saw him at the festival," Valerie said, trying to catch Solomon's gaze. "It wasn't him. It couldn't have been. He's not the Wolf."

"I want him interrogated," Solomon said to his soldiers, ignoring Valerie. "Look at him, the way he's crouched there...."

Solomon had a point. Claude looked small from where they stood, but he didn't look innocent. He looked wild, like a fledgling vulture left to fend for itself in an abandoned nest of twigs and human hair.

But, Valerie wondered, what would be an appropriate reaction? He was responding the way they all should have been. Why were they complacent in the face of the tragedy and brutality that had descended on them? What mechanism allowed these things to be glossed over?

But even his own mother would not stand up for him. Marguerite sat below on a stack of hay, dazed. She could not look up, could only gaze at her own hands and wonder what would become of her sweet, strange boy. She had never known what to do with him, had never asked for him, and so absolved herself of any blame.

"His speech is twisted," Solomon pronounced. "He communes with demons. He practices the dark arts. *He's a conjurer.*"

The great Father Solomon, Valerie realized, had only a schoolboy's simplistic understanding of humanity. He thought of people as predator and prey, good and evil. He couldn't allow room for ambiguity. That which was not pure must be impure.

But she had given in to such simpleminded idiocy just today—suspecting her grandmother, suspecting Peter. Her cheeks burned with shame.

"He's not evil. I *know* him!" she cried out, indicting herself even as she challenged Solomon.

"Better than I knew my own wife?" Solomon finally turned to face her.

And Valerie had no answer to that.

Solomon held out a battered tarot card: The Fool, a barefooted beggar.

"Look. This was found near the body of your dead sister."

"He performed magic," Madame Lazar stepped in, materializing from the crowd. "I knew it was the Devil's work!"

Valerie looked incredulously at Madame Lazar. *If there ever was a witch...*

"He's different," Valerie said, looking up at the boy in question. His eyes shimmered like water. "That doesn't make him guilty."

"Innocent people don't run. He must be running from something," the old witch replied.

"If the innocent are unjust, I'd rather be counted among the guilty."

Madame Lazar turned and scowled, suddenly mistrustful of Valerie.

Solomon looked to the masked bowman. "Get him down from there."

Roxanne launched herself again at Solomon, but the masked bowman swatted her away like a fly.

Two soldiers turned down the hinged spurs on their boots and pulled out their hand scythes. They hooked their fingers between the slats, ascending like insects.

"Don't startle him!" Roxanne cried out. It was a long drop.

Seeing them coming, Claude ducked under the grain chute. It seemed for a moment that he would fall, but he righted his posture only to find himself cornered on the top platform.

As the soldiers took hold of him, Roxanne caught Father Auguste by the arm. He looked nervously indecisive, like a young child who'd been offered too many choices. He did not know anymore whose side he was on.

"Do something, *please*," Roxanne tried.

But Father Auguste just stared ahead and did not respond. He stood aside to allow the soldiers to pass by, dragging a wriggling Claude between them. It seemed he had chosen his side.

Roxanne collapsed on the ground, sobbing.

Valerie felt something she hadn't felt since she was seven years old.

Utter helplessness.

21

The soldiers dragged Claude into a ruined barn behind the granary and then dropped his limp body to the ground. His glittering graphite eyes opened to see a grotesque, majestic shape looming over him. The metal elephant.

Claude cried out, for the sake of the cries themselves, knowing they would effect no change. Frantically, he tried to scuttle away from the torture device. Anything but that. He made it to the far wall and huddled in the corner, mumbling hurriedly to himself in a wet whisper.

Solomon, who had been trailing behind, doubting that Claude could actually be the Wolf, entered the barn. Still, he couldn't show weakness. Father Auguste had followed him in.

"Do not touch him"—his eyes were small like pebbles as he finished the sentence—"until I order you to."

Claude's chanting sped up.

"Now..." Solomon continued, breaking into a grim smile. He raised one arm so that his robes hung down like a black velvet wing, and pointed one sharpened finger toward the brazen elephant. "You may touch him."

The soldiers could make out Claude's rhyme through his sobs: *"There was a boy, his name was Claude, different and alone, but close to God."*

"Silence, monster," a soldier barked, clopping him on the back of his head. Petrified, Claude held his fist to his mouth. His eyes darted around, but there was nowhere to go. He set his weight into his heels and his heels against the ground. But it was not enough. He was seized by huge, gripping hands and dragged toward the torture chamber.

Father Solomon came closer and gazed down at him.

"Tell me the name of the Wolf."

Claude simply shook, too terrified to understand what he was being asked.

Solomon nodded, and the soldiers shoved Claude toward the hulking torture chamber.

But something was stuck, and the men could not turn the crank that opened the door in the side of the elephant.

"Can't get it," one of the soldiers said, moving aside to let the other try his luck with the handle. It gave.

As the door was cranked open, the two soldiers picked

up Claude by the arms and legs and heaved him in. Then they cranked the door shut again.

"Tell me the name," Solomon spoke at the brazen beast. No reply.

"What are you doing?" One soldier turned to the other, who was already lighting a fire below the elephant.

"I'm doing as I've been told to do," he whispered shortly. "And you, sir, would be wise to as well." The soldiers stepped back, one reluctantly, one in grim resolution.

As the flames flickered at the bronze belly, the sound of Claude thrashing echoed from within the metallic monster.

"Listen to how he sings of his love of Satan...."

Father Solomon felt Father Auguste's horrified stare. Observant people know when they're being observed.

Solomon took a deep breath, rearing back with it, like a cat about to pounce. He moved to the side of the village priest. "What men like you and me do, we do for the greater good. As men of the cloth, it is our burden to rid the world of its evils."

"Tell me." Auguste feebly tried to stand strong. "What could possibly be the good of this?"

Father Solomon leaned close so that Auguste could make no mistake about the level of his resolve.

"I killed my wife to protect my children." He let his words have their full effect. "Our methods of pleasing God are sometimes flawed, Father, but such is the business of werewolf hunting. You'd best develop a stomach for it."

"What are you saying, Father?" Auguste replied in such a dangerous voice, powerful in its quiet, audible over the cries and thumps, that Solomon had no choice but to stop and turn. He held a finger to the other man's lips.

"I'm saying that you must make a choice. And I suggest, for your safety, that you join me."

He turned to the soldiers. "Do not release the boy until he offers the name of the Wolf." Then he swept out of the building.

"How can he speak? He's being tortured," Father Auguste said quietly to himself, hoping that Father Solomon knew what he was doing but worrying he might not.

Solomon was the only customer in the tavern. The man of God was drinking down his midday meal. How else to still the anger he felt at these ignorant peasants who did nothing but work against themselves?

He looked up from his drink as the Captain entered, followed by a village girl. Solomon narrowed his eyes, sure he knew her.

Ah, yes. The boy's sister. The redhead with the sweet face. She was girlish and God-fearing; he liked that. Solomon did not object as the Captain brought her forward.

"Yes, child." He acknowledged her presence.

"I have come to bargain for Claude's release." She said her well-rehearsed line aloud.

When Solomon didn't say anything, she thrust her closed hand over the table in front of him. She opened her fist, and it sounded as though she'd dropped a few coins. She pulled her hand back, as though from the heat of a fire, and Solomon could see that she had indeed. A few paltry pieces of silver.

His lips tightened; it was not clear whether he was angry or trying to stifle laughter.

"What do you mean me to do with this?" Solomon asked.

"I..."

"With this, I could buy one loaf of rye or a half-dozen eggs. Thank you for that gift. Now tell me," he said, coming close enough that she felt the touch of his cool breath. "What were you hoping to *bargain* with?"

Roxanne slid the coins off the table and back into her hand. They seemed dirty now. Her face burning red, she managed to get out, "I have more than money."

Father Solomon raised his eyebrows.

She lowered her shawl and loosened her blouse until she was very nearly exposed and offered him the shockingly full breasts, which she had always kept carefully hidden.

Solomon sneered at the exposed flesh, insulted.

"This is your idea of a bribe?" Solomon's brow was still lifted.

The Captain laughed roundly. They let her stand there, feeling hopelessly foolish.

"Don't you want me?" she murmured, almost convincingly.

"Turn around, girl," Solomon spat out.

Now it was she who felt dirty. Roxanne managed to cover herself before the Captain laid his hands on her to drag her out.

"*Wait!*" she cried.

The worst thing Roxanne had ever had to do was beat the body of a filthy, drunken man off her mother with Claude standing nearby, wringing his hands as he witnessed the scene. This was so much worse. This...this would haunt her forever. But she had no choice.

"Wait, please. I do have one more thing." She spoke quickly enough that she could not turn back.

"If you spare my brother," she began, "I'll give you the name of a witch."

This got Solomon's attention. "Now *that* is worth something."

Valerie's father was keeping watch by the fire while Suzette rested, delirious in bed. This meant that he had fallen asleep, slumped slack-jawed on a stool, an axe lying dormant across his lap. It was the same size axe as everyone else's, the same one he'd always used, and yet it looked too large for him. She noticed the sunken plum-colored pits beneath his closed eyes and settled beside him to do the watching herself.

As Valerie had walked home from the granary, stunned by what she'd seen, she spied the three little girls whom Lucie used to take care of. They were seated, pallid and still, at a cottage window, watching with vacant stares and pursed lips as Valerie passed. Valerie wondered if, in a year or two, they would even remember Lucie. Her sweet generosity, the way she'd twirled them one at a time, giving one a second turn because she wanted it and then giving all a second turn because fair was fair. Would they remember that?

Amidst the chaos, deep mistrust was growing underneath like mold. The villagers' eyes glazed over, so they did not really see each other.

Some men had assembled a small group, a vigilante brigade that knocked on doors, seeking anything that was out of the ordinary. And they found things, too, in just the few hours they had been searching. One villager kept an assortment of feathers by her bed. Another had a book in an ancient language, despite claiming to not be able to read. Someone else had given birth despite being past the usual age for such a thing.

Yes, they found things.

They had a hard time, though, getting Solomon's soldiers to listen, as the soldiers seemed to have their own way of doing things. So the men stored the information away for later.

Lost in such thoughts, Valerie had drifted off, too. But now both father and daughter awakened to pounding at the door—*Bang! Bang!*—then pounding that tore into the door itself. Something was coming in.

Valerie pictured those great claws working furiously at the wood, those huge teeth ripping out chunks.

The frayed wood of the door flew apart—but the Wolf didn't burst into the room. It was a pair of soldiers who charged in and took command of the space, staking claim over everything. One kicked over a chair that was not in his way, just because there was no reason not to. The people were theirs, too. They shoved Cesaire aside and grabbed hold of Valerie, dragging her off.

Suzette never even woke up.

"Tell them what you told me," Solomon demanded, leaning across the bar in the tavern.

Roxanne was seated directly across from Valerie but did not look at her, staring through her to the wall behind.

The tavern had hastily been made into a courtroom, the benches assembled into pews, and when there were no more benches, people used stools. Valerie was tied to a chair for all to see at the front of the room. Heavily equipped soldiers kept guard at every exit, standing stiffly in their armor.

Valerie had seen Peter enter, seen how hard it was for him to be there, to see her like that. He stood alone in the farthest corner.

Roxanne knew she had to respond, that people were waiting to hear what she'd promised them. She summoned her courage, her voice shaky.

"She can climb the tallest trees," she began, repeating dutifully what she had told Solomon, what she believed to be the truth, a truth that fractured her heart to believe. "She can run faster than all the girls. She wears this red cloak. The Devil's color," she added, for those who couldn't put it together.

The rope dug into Valerie's skin as Roxanne continued. "And she can talk to werewolves. I've seen it with my own eyes."

Valerie heard the villagers let out a communal gasp as, beneath her red hair, Roxanne's face turned pink with tears. Valerie quivered with her own heartbreak as she watched her friend go through with it.

"Do you deny the allegations?" Solomon turned to Valerie with mock incredulity.

Valerie felt wooden. "No."

The crowd murmured.

"I don't deny it."

Prudence sat poised and silent. Her mother had curled up into the end of the pew and was chewing her hair. Henry was seated between a friend and his grandmother, dressed in her mourning black. Rose was seated right behind Henry, still trying to be noticed, even now. Peter still stood alone.

"And what was the *nature* of this conversation?" Solomon steepled his fingers.

Valerie, happy to find that she still had a glimmer of humor left, held back a faint smile. She would give him the information, but in the order she wanted to tell it. "The Wolf said"—she paused to draw it out—"that you don't know what you're dealing with."

Feeling the eyes in the room shift over to him, Solomon smiled showily; he was too smart to fall into that trap.

"I'm sure that it did," he said sweetly. "What *else* did it say?"

Valerie felt as if her head were full of wool, the way she felt when she was sick with a cold. She felt separated from her own body.

"It promised to leave Daggorhorn in peace. But only if I leave with it," Valerie thought, only to find that she had said it aloud.

Roxanne's body reacted, her shock stemming the tears her will hadn't managed to hold back.

Valerie felt Peter's eyes boring into her from the back of the room.

A heavy quiet overtook the room. Solomon thought a moment. This was better than he'd hoped. He leaned in close to Valerie, as though no one else were there.

"The Wolf is someone in this village who wants you, Valerie," he said in the voice he reserved for the public. "Do you know who it is? I'd think very hard if I were you."

Valerie was, of course, silent. She did not know anything for certain, and she could not tell. She looked again to gauge Peter's reaction. But he was no longer there.

Solomon was an astute observer. He knew Valerie well enough by now; he would get nothing more.

"It wants *her*, not you," he appealed to the villagers, trying a different tactic. "Save yourselves. It's very simple. We give the Wolf what it wants."

Henry leapt to his feet. His friend looked up at him

unhappily; Henry's dogmatic adherence to his principles had always bothered those around him, as it meant that he was more plodding, less fun than he might have been. He would not race off with an old woman's undergarments, snatched from a hanging clothesline, or swap a pawn for a bishop in a chess game. But this time he was putting himself in danger.

"We cannot give her to the Wolf. That's human sacrifice."

"We've all made sacrifices," Madame Lazar spoke up in her noncommittal way, as though she were merely making an observation.

Henry scanned the room, seeking support where there was none. The villagers were never so united as when they were banded against someone.

Desperate, Henry spun around to where he had seen Peter standing earlier. Gone, his post abandoned.

Valerie was touched by Henry's effort, even though she sensed that it was more about doing what was right than about her. At least he had stood up to Father Solomon. Not even Valerie's family had done that.

Her parents and her grandmother sat together, afraid to speak up. They would not offer themselves up now; what good would it do to be locked up together? There would have to be another way.

Her mother still looked ill from her attack, and Valerie wasn't even sure Suzette was entirely conscious. Cesaire looked angry but trapped, as if he finally grasped his own powerlessness. And Grandmother—well, Valerie hoped she might have a plan, but she also knew that the woman would be risking her own life to speak now. She was grateful, at least, that Roxanne had not brought Grandmother into it.

Solomon, always a man of action, took the opportunity to nod to the soldiers, who tramped over to untie Valerie and relocate her. The trial was over.

The villagers were eager to escape the room, which felt bitter with the aftertaste of their decision, their conviction that they deserved to live more than Valerie did. So they filed out wordlessly, holding their chatter until they were out of doors. No one dared to speak to Father Solomon; no one dared to look at him. No one wanted to stand out from the rest.

Only Father Auguste hung back to say a word to Father Solomon.

"I thought you came to *kill* the Wolf, not to appease it."

Solomon looked at him as though doing so were a taxing trial of his patience.

"I have no intention of appeasing it," he said conspiratorially. "The girl is merely the bait for our trap tonight."

"Of course, of course," Father Auguste murmured. He stepped back, his faith restored, pacified in leaving his hero to do his hero's work. Auguste hadn't even thought of that! He turned away, feeling he had done his duty, pleased with the order of things. Valerie saw that he would not take any blame, either. She was alone in this.

The villagers had gathered in small, tightly knit groups just outside the tavern door. Cesaire, Suzette, and Grandmother stepped out and into the aftermath of the hearing, the bubbling of talk subsiding at the sight of them, especially of Grandmother, who was not often at village events.

Madame Lazar, though, continued to speak loudly to Rose and a group of gossipy women. "...Her grandmother lives all alone in the woods."

Though it was not the first time she had heard such prejudice, something made Grandmother stop to listen.

"The first victim was her sister. The second was her fiancé's father. And don't forget her poor mother, scarred for life," she alleged loudly. "If the girl isn't a witch, then how do you explain it?"

Cesaire saw that Grandmother was falling under the trance of Madame Lazar's voice. Something about it seemed to resonate with her.

"Don't listen to her."

"She's not wrong," Grandmother mused. "Valerie *is* at the center of this."

Cesaire looked concerned but only nodded and started Suzette down the road to put her back in bed. Grandmother paused to catch the last word.

"I've tried to talk Henry out of his feelings for her," Madame Lazar went on, her eyes droopy at the corners.

"But there's no hope. He's lost his senses. If that doesn't sound like witchcraft to you…" Madame Lazar trailed off, her listeners nodding their agreement.

No one spoke to Henry when he pushed out of the tavern to confront Peter, who was standing across the way, watching the crowd from a shadowy corner. Peter straightened from his lean, ready for the fight.

"What was that about?" Henry's voice came out higher than he would have liked.

"Shh." Peter's eyes shifted around the square.

"I thought you cared about her," Henry said, careful to steady his voice this time.

Peter rubbed his eyes and then opened them, hoping to find that Henry had gone. He hadn't.

"I *do* care." Peter sighed, seeing that he would have to give a genuine answer, that Henry wouldn't take anything less. "But"—Peter nodded in the direction of the tavern, where the Captain was—"*I'm* trying to be smart about it."

Henry looked quickly and saw that even his brisk glance had not escaped the Captain's notice.

"You're going to rescue her." Henry understood at last.

Peter didn't bother to respond.

Henry studied his rival. He felt that he could trust him but thought that he'd rather not. And yet Henry was not so prideful that he would sacrifice the girl he loved. He watched as a soldier hauled Valerie out of the tavern, taking her elsewhere to be locked up. Seeing where the ropes had chafed her skin red and raw, he found it was easy to reach a decision.

"I'll help you."

"I'm not that desperate," Peter answered coldly, *his* pride apparently still intact.

"Oh, really? What's your plan, then?"

Peter shifted his weight.

"You don't have one, do you? Look, the blacksmith shop is mine now," he reminded him. "I've got tools and the skills to use them. You need me." Henry wanted the satisfaction of Peter giving in. "Admit it."

Peter didn't like it. But he liked the idea of letting Valerie be taken by the Wolf even less. He knew it *would* be easier with Henry's help.

"Fine." As he thought through it, Peter's face lightened, but it was subtle, almost imperceptible, like the gradation of tones in a shadow. He didn't necessarily need to trust Henry, just trust that Henry's love for Valerie was strong.

But what if it was too strong? Supernaturally strong?

"If you're the Wolf, though, I'll chop off your head and piss down the hole."

"And I'll do the same for you. With pleasure."

"Fair enough."

The two men looked at each other searchingly, amazed at the truce they had reached, uneasy though it was.

Roxanne, feeling hollow, eaten by corruption from the inside out, approached the Captain.

"Where's my brother? Father Solomon told me he would be released." She sniffled in the cold.

Something indiscernible crossed the Captain's face.

"Released." He nodded absently. "Yes. I believe he was."

The Captain turned and swept back inside the tavern. Roxanne assumed that the motion meant she ought to follow. She hurried after him as he easily took the stairs three at a time. He led her through the tavern and out the back to a wheelbarrow standing in the yard. Roxanne was confused, and she paused to look around. She didn't see her brother.

The Captain shooed away a few gently pecking crows

and lifted the handles to turn the wheelbarrow in her direction. Roxanne saw the load was covered with a blanket. As it was wheeled toward her, a hand fell free. Claude's hand.

Roxanne shook her head, backing away.

The Captain stopped just in front of her and uncovered the body as Roxanne fell to her knees on the soggy ground.

Claude's skin was sheet white, met by the cold, and his freckles were stark in contrast. His skin had been blistered on his hands and feet, his face bruised and swollen.

It hadn't occurred to her that she might not find Claude alive; even though she'd sunk to depths she could never before have imagined, still something *so* horrible had not even crossed her mind.

Earlier that week, floorboards had creaked. Cupboards had refused to latch closed. People were poor and food scarce. There was jealousy and meanness and vanity.

Things hadn't been perfect. But they had been bearable.

Now, evil had descended upon Daggorhorn.

24

J ust two days earlier, Valerie could not have imagined she would be here. Everyone she loved had turned against her, or else she had turned against them. Her sister had died. And tonight she would die, too.

She had been thrown into a prison cell. It was damp and dark, as though she were already in her grave. It was normally used to hold animals, but the locked iron bars across the top would look at home in any jail. A few sparse candles cast sharp shadows onto the walls. The guards had at least provided some light.

But what did it matter? She had no one. No one had spoken up in her defense.

Except Henry, whose love she had crushed for the love of

another. And that someone else had fled the room. Peter had not even stayed to stand up for her.

Henry would find someone else to marry. He would come to love Rose or Prudence or a girl from a neighboring village. But she knew Peter would find no one, would think of her always, would hold her somewhere no one could reach. He would protect his memory of her as he had these past ten years, saving her for himself.

She wished she hadn't turned him away when he came to her door. If only she had gone with him.

She heard a rustling from the dark and then saw her grandmother's face peering in at her. So perhaps she wasn't entirely alone.

"Tell me, darling," Grandmother asked, her voice sorrowful, "is there anything you need?"

The elk-horn knife flashed in Valerie's mind. She had tucked it into her boot while Cesaire was sleeping. She wished she could show her grandmother, but the guard's eyes never roamed away for long.

Valerie's shoulders trembled as a chill rattled through her. Solomon had taken her red cloak, a violation somehow more brutal than the rest. She needed many things, but she knew it was pointless to ask. The guard would never let anything be passed down to her.

"No." She shook her head.

Valerie hadn't yet given up the hope that her grandmother had not spoken up in the courtroom because she had another plan, but she realized that, like everyone else, she was just afraid. Not of the Wolf but of a man. Solomon.

"Listen." Grandmother lowered her voice. "The Wolf never used to attack in the open like it did at the festival. Why show itself now?"

"Maybe it's this moon...."

"It wants you. And it wanted your sister." Grandmother tried to work through the logic out loud.

My sister.

"It might have killed randomly at the festival to hide the fact that the first killing wasn't random at all," Grandmother speculated.

Valerie wasn't sure what Grandmother was getting at.

"No. The Wolf didn't choose Lucie. She must have offered herself to the Wolf." Valerie swallowed, forcing herself to say it aloud. "I didn't know it then, but she was in love with Henry. Rose thinks she heard about my engagement, and the only option she saw left was to take her own life." But even as she said it, the story didn't ring true.

"Lucie loved Henry...." Grandmother paused. "But that she would take her own life is inconceivable. Impossible. She wouldn't do that." Grandmother seemed to have developed another theory. She moved closer to the bars to speak further.

But the clanking of keys came first, the guard moving to stand over her, a towering presence.

"Visit's up."

At the other end of the village, Cesaire scooped out a chalky handful of corn and scattered the kernels in front of the chickens. Ordinarily, this was Suzette's job, but she was still resting, afraid of risking infection. Cesaire was glad to be given a task, some way to make his body useful other than standing guard over his wife, whom he had ceased to love. His daughters were gone, and all he had left to do was care for a few thankless chickens.

Everyone had gone home after the trial, wrecked from stress and fear. A few people were outside, women pounding laundry with big paddles, men moving logs. Routine helped. Death, it seemed, had not settled fully over the village, as life was still being lived. All was not over yet.

Cesaire noticed Peter making his way toward him from down the street, pushing a wheelbarrow loaded with a wooden barrel. Cesaire continued pawing through the corn as he watched, coating his palm with a dusty white residue. The men stood apart as the wheels came to a creaking stop.

"I'm going to save your daughter." Peter spoke first, watching for Cesaire's reaction. "And then I intend to marry her. I would like your blessing in this, but I can live without it."

There was a moment of silence. Peter had said what he needed to say and turned to go. But then Cesaire stepped forward and reached out to embrace him, both men heartened by the moment of human custom in the midst of unearthly chaos.

T he wind blew open the door of the blacksmith
shop, and Grandmother rushed in with it. The
shop was in a state of cluttered disarray.

"Hello, Henry."

Henry didn't even bother to turn away from the flames.
Not for a woman who wouldn't speak up for her own
granddaughter.

"We're closed."

"I want to thank you for speaking up today," she said,
ignoring his proclamation. "That was very brave."

"I only said what I felt." Henry was forging something in
the fire. The thing he brought out glowed bright white, like
a fallen piece of the moon. Gripping it with a set of tongs,

he began cranking a lever up and down and set it on a corner to shape it.

"You are under no obligation to stand in Valerie's defense." Grandmother spoke to Henry's back. "You've already broken off the engagement."

"She's in love with someone else." Henry gritted his teeth, resentful that she was making him say it. He had begun hammering the piece into a point. "That doesn't mean I stopped caring about her."

"I imagine that's the same way Lucie felt about you."

Henry shrugged, uneasy at the mention of her name. "I've been told she thought she was in love with me."

"Yes, Valerie just told me."

Henry finished splicing the ends off his creation. He didn't have much time.

"It seems Lucie would have done anything for you. She would even have met you on a Wolf night, if you'd asked her to."

He wiped his hands on his apron. "I don't see what that has to do with anything," he said shortly, trying to keep his voice civil.

Just as he said it, though, he understood, his confusion morphing into anger. He finally looked at her. "You think I'm the Wolf."

Grandmother stood up straighter.

"Do you realize what you are accusing me of? Murder!"

"I'm not *accusing* anyone of anything," she said, knowing otherwise. In the heat of the shop, Grandmother was wilting, her accusations losing their focus, their intensity. "I'm trying to find out the truth," she continued anyway.

As she said this, though, Henry's face shifted. It emptied of anger, becoming soft again with wonder and then settling into horror—but also with a certain delight that he could now accuse his accuser.

There was a jarring clatter as Henry let his tool drop and stepped toward her, almost seductively.

"It's *you*," he said, pointing at her, stabbing his finger into the air. "My God, it's you. I can smell it on you now."

Grandmother became nervous, having exhausted her evidence against him. "What can you smell on me?" She stepped closer to the door.

"The night my father died, I could smell the Wolf. A deep musk." Henry moved even closer. "The same scent I smell on you at this exact moment."

Henry was standing very near now, his eyes burning. His breath was on her, and she felt faint with the heat from the fire, from his accusation.

"What were you doing out there in that cabin? All by yourself?" Henry did not let up. "On the night your granddaughter was *murdered*?"

In that moment, the smell flashed across Grandmother's senses like a long-forgotten name. But that was enough. The young man was right. She felt the urgent need to defend herself.

"Henry, I read until I fell asleep." Confused, she clung to her alibi.

"And then what?"

Grandmother was quiet. The scent rose off her clothes like fog off a river. It was bitter and penetrating.

"You don't know, do you?" he pressed her.

She had to get out of there. She had to get home and check something. She had to know for sure. How had her suspicions been echoed back at her so easily?

She edged out the open door, letting it slam shut behind her.

26

In the twilight, the three men worked together in the same way that young children play, beside one another but without interacting. They didn't want to attract attention.

Peter glanced up from his work. He was glad to see Cesaire pushing the wheelbarrow around the square, Henry busy at work in the blacksmith shop. The plan was in action.

As Cesaire pushed, the wheelbarrow dripped translucent lamp oil into the dirty snow. He paused briefly to have a taste of his flask, taking the moment to look around. He noted, wincing, that the Captain was keeping watch across the square. Maintaining an easy expression, Cesaire casually continued pushing along. But the Captain was headed for him anyway, with two soldiers in tow.

Cesaire's body made the decision for him. *Run*.

Slogging through the muddy slush, he knocked aside a few pheasant crates and leapt over a dough trough.

The Captain pulled out a long whip and snapped it at the fleeing Cesaire. The whip only licked him, but down he went, face-first into a snowdrift. He attempted to crawl away but made it only a few uneven steps before he was tackled and seized by faceless, gripping hands.

"A precaution," a soldier spat out. "We don't want any trouble from the witch's family."

There were footsteps, and then Father Solomon's voice emerged from the darkness.

"Put on your harlot's robe." His voice was hoarse as he waited while the hatch was opened, and then he tossed Valerie her crimson cloak.

She draped the beautiful fabric over herself; it felt soft and smooth. A soldier appeared and clamped her into iron manacles; they twirled loose around her thin wrists. Then Valerie saw that someone else was approaching. It was her father, forced to stoop under the low ceiling.

"Valerie." He stopped in front of her. "I tried to protect you. You and Lucie..."

Lucie. She seemed imaginary now, almost mythical. Made-up.

"It's all right, Papa," she said, choking on the words. "You taught us to be strong."

Valerie realized how lonely he would be when she was dead.

"You're my good girl. Stay strong."

She felt that hand on her, that grip as tight as it ever was, and knew that she was feeling it for the last time.

Valerie could feel her heart rising up her throat. What could she say? She was almost grateful when the soldier slammed Cesaire aside and nudged her toward where Solomon was waiting.

The mask was made of such heavy iron that it was almost impossible to keep one's head up while wearing it. It had only small openings for eyes. Its conelike snout was unmistakably that of a wolf's. The muzzle was a toothy grin made of sharpened inlaid ivory. Designed to maximize public humiliation, the wolf mask was a tour de force of human cruelty, and Valerie could see the satisfaction in Father Solomon's face as the Captain fitted it over her head.

Then all she saw was darkness, and all she felt was the weight of metal, jerked around as it was secured with buckles and snaps.

At first, she had struggled against the cruel embrace of the manacle chain, pulling away from it, but it bit fast into her wrists. So Valerie staggered more quickly down the village street, blindly pulled along by the horse, unwilling to give the villagers the satisfaction of seeing her fall.

It was hot inside the mask, and Valerie's forehead was slick where it met the metal. The mask slid and wobbled as she moved falteringly through the slush on the ground.

In the fading light, villagers had assembled to gape at the macabre parade, unable to turn away as it plodded slowly down the street. The last night of the blood moon approached.

A bystander or two muttered just audibly, "Witch." Others moved their hands absentmindedly to make the sign of the cross against themselves.

A voice that she recognized as Madame Lazar's called out, "Not so pretty now, is she?" A moment later, Rose's voice came, calling her a witch and worse things, assuring Madame Lazar that her grandson would find a suitable wife. She sounded as though she'd never known Valerie at all.

Valerie felt someone tugging at her hair and tried not to scream as he or she yanked at her. A moment later, her blond locks were jerked free by a soldier who was impatient to keep the train of shame moving forward.

Chained now to a post, kneeling on the sacrificial altar, Valerie heard Father Auguste's voice above her, blessing her, rustling pages in his Bible. A moment later, there came a familiar voice in an unfamiliar strangled cry.

"That's my baby!"

With some effort, Valerie lifted the iron weight of her head. Through the tiny eyes of the mask, Valerie saw her mother, barefoot, fluttering in a frenzy like a dying moth. Her streaked face, raised into welts wherever there wasn't an open sore, looked like it was smeared with jam. It had healed in places but hadn't in others. It was lumpy, the wounds deep.

She stopped in front of Solomon.

"Let her go, you bastard!"

Suzette's hair was in clumps, and she smelled sour. "Let her go!" she ranted. She reached up to strike Solomon, but he effortlessly caught her wrist.

The village was speechless. They didn't like to see her like this, out of control, a madwoman. Another casualty. Even Father Solomon did not say anything for a few moments, letting her rage.

Valerie couldn't look anymore and rested the iron muzzle against her chest.

"You should go home," she heard Solomon say, like a disappointed father. "You should all go home."

Frightened villagers reached out to Valerie's sagging mother, pulling her back. Suzette covered her face with

her hands as they steered her toward home. It was too
much to bear.

Hours passed. Darkness fell.

Valerie looked up at the blood moon. It was the final
night. She had heard the village doors lock and shutters
slam shut. Light-headed now, she wished she could lie down
and sleep away the hours, but the chains held her upright.

A dark shape loomed over her. She gasped, a hollow
sound in the echoing metal mask. She closed her eyes and
waited for the end to come.

"Valerie," said a girl's voice.

She opened her eyes, angling to see out of the eyeholes.

The shape leaned into view.

"Prudence?"

"Roxanne wanted you to know that she's sorry. She only
said those things to save her brother," Prudence whispered.

"I know that." Valerie shook with a chill that rattled her
chains. "Will you tell her that I forgive her?"

"Of course. But I wanted to say...I don't know what
to say."

There was an uneven cadence in Prudence's tone.

"You don't have to say anything."

"No, I want to."

Valerie tried to lean forward, her chains going taut with
the effort. Prudence bent from her upright posture, hinged

forward. Her brown hair fell around her face like a curtain.

"I want you to know that you may have fooled Roxanne, but you don't fool me," she said, her words hissing like fire. "You always thought you were better than us; too good even for Henry! Your loss is our gain. Now you're going to get what you deserve."

"Prudence." Suddenly, Valerie could not recall what it had been like when Prudence was her friend. She tried to be strong. "I think you'd better go." Her eyes felt dry, like peeled fruit that had been left out overnight.

Prudence looked up. The clouds had pulled apart, revealing the crimson moon again. "Yes. You're right. It won't be long now. The Wolf is coming for you."

Valerie was almost grateful for her mask then, as it betrayed nothing of what she felt to her tormentor. She closed her eyes, and when she opened them again, Prudence was gone.

A winter wind howled, and Valerie's shivers rattled her chains.

There was nothing to do but wait. The Wolf would come for her.

But then what?

Across the square, Solomon was standing atop the granary tower, surrounded by weapons, ropes, and quivers. Below, soldiers were hiding in alleys, guarding the horses, sharpening silver-tipped arrows, waiting in windows.

All was set and ready. Nothing left to do but clean his fingernails with the tip of a knife and flick the unclean specks to the floor. His skin, healed slightly, was tearing at its seams like a baked apple. Father Auguste joined him at his side.

"Do you know how you kill a tiger, Father Auguste?" Father Solomon asked, whispering stonily, looking down at the pathetic rag-doll figure of Valerie chained to the altar. "You tie out your best goat and wait."

Near the crumbling town wall, a dark figure crouched, searching by torchlight for something in the snow. He found what he was seeking and lowered the torch flame. Nothing happened for a moment.

But then the ground caught fire and traced a blazing line into the square, picking up speed as it shot across the trail of lamp oil to the abandoned barn and the stack of kindling laid there earlier for just this purpose. Peter stayed low with his torch, his face lit by the flames, watching with satisfaction as the results of his work and Cesaire's took shape.

From his command post atop the granary tower, Solomon squinted against the sudden light, watching the flame and smoke fill the square below. He let out a whispered curse. There was no time for this, not tonight. He signaled to the Captain — and in an instant, his men were rappelling down the granary wall into the square.

From his command post atop the granary tower, Solomon squinted against the sudden light, watching the flame and smoke fill the square below. He let out a whispered curse. There was no time for this, not tonight. He signaled to the Captain — and in an instant, his men were rappelling down the granary wall into the square.

The close inner space of the mask filled with light, and Valerie looked out through her eyeholes, mystified by the flames and the smoke swirling in the wind. She jerked against her bonds in surprise when she heard a voice close behind her.

"I'm going to get you out of here."

Even in the chaos, she knew it was Henry. But he was different. The power of his intensity, the feverishness of his concentration, frightened her.

"What's happening?" she asked, confused.

"It's part of the plan. I'm going to get you out of here," he repeated. He liked the sound of his own words. It was he, not Peter, doing the actual freeing. His hands went to work with the strange keys he had made earlier in the day—skeleton keys. He had practiced, and his fingers did the work for him, the key grinding in the lock, probing for the tumblers.

As he leaned in close, all Valerie could see, filling the eyeholes of her mask, were his brown eyes, glimmering in the flames. Sharply intelligent. Burning.

Exactly like the Wolf's.

Valerie thought of what her grandmother had started to suggest. She thought of the note that was in Lucie's hands. Someone must have written it. Then she thought of her elk-horn knife.

Click. One lock sprang open. Two more to go.

From his crouch by the wall, Peter saw the soldiers kicking snow over the flames, stomping it out. Staring through the smoke, he could just make out the two figures at the altar. Henry hadn't freed Valerie yet. *What is taking him so long?*

Henry got to be the face of the operation. Valerie would think of herself as indebted to him always for saving her life, would forever consider him the mastermind, the way even the playwright leaves the theater thinking the actor invented his own lines.

Henry the hero. Damn.

We're on the same side, he reminded himself. Peter scanned the base of the granary, knowing he had to buy Henry some time.

Click. The second lock popped open.

Valerie's hands were free.

One more to go.

Henry's fingers worked on the mask without thinking, the way a musician's fingers find the strings themselves on a song he has played often. But, desperately probing, he couldn't loosen the clasp. He muttered angrily. Valerie's free hand felt stealthily for her knife. It would be just like the Wolf to come under the guise of a rescue. Wouldn't it?

Whack!

Peter swung his axe from behind, using the handle to

take down the soldier standing guard at the door of the granary. Without hesitation, he heaved his torch in through the granary door, but before he could see if the flames found their target, his legs gave way under him.

Peter looked down, surprised, and saw that he'd been ensnared in a weighted chain that someone had tossed through the air. In an instant, the chain-wielding soldier was upon him.

Hawkeyed, Solomon never wavered his gaze from the smoke, looking for movement at the altar. The girl was still there, that much he could see, but no sign of the Wolf yet. Was it possible these village morons were making a fool of him?

He heard a snap. It was a small sound, but it was a sound nonetheless.

And then he heard another.

He sniffed the air and knew right away. The granary, too, was on fire. Someone would pay for the night's sloppiness.

"Evacuate," he commanded his soldiers.

He led the way down the spiral stairs of the tower, breathing in the thick, smoky air. It made him heady. As he turned a curve, he froze—through a window, he saw a twitch of movement at the altar, something slight.

Just what he'd feared.

The granary trembled around him, and the walls began to give way, the columns toasted and crumbling, flames ejecting into the night.

"There," Solomon said to the bowman behind him.

The bowman and Father Auguste looked where he did. The smoke had cleared enough to show someone, a man in a cloak, crouched by Valerie, removing the wolf mask.

The bowman raised his crossbow but hesitated as a beam came crashing to the ground.

"Wait! Stop!" Father Auguste cried, his hands clasped together as though he were holding on to something precious.

"Do it," Solomon ordered.

The bowman took aim at Henry from the window. A stationary target, an easy shot...

But as he triggered the bow, something blurred across his vision, something close enough to make him flinch and send the bolt off course.

It was Father Auguste, who had seen enough barbarity at last and jumped at the bowman's line of aim, ruining the shot.

"*Run!*" Father Auguste shouted toward the altar, waving his Bible in the air.

His one syllable resonated through the air like the chime of a bell.

Solomon didn't waste time. He swung his arm and plunged his dagger into Auguste's chest.

The two men locked eyes. Father Auguste's went wide

with shock and pain and then emptied of life. He crumpled to the ground, his Bible fallen facedown at his side.

Solomon's eyes shot back to the altar. The wolf mask was left abandoned on its side. He knew the moment had passed. Another beam fell.

"We should go," he said calmly.

Outside, he found that his soldiers had taken on a prisoner.

"This one started the fire." The stronger of the two soldiers thrust Peter forward. He was in manacles. They'd treated him roughly; they didn't appreciate being made to look ridiculous by a street boy.

"Our men found him wrestling with a soldier," the other spoke up.

"Lock him in the elephant. We'll light it later." Solomon's voice was like a crystal, cut with disgust as he moved into the smoldering square.

"The witch has escaped!" Valerie could hear the shouts as she ran.

It was hard to comprehend that they were shouting about her, impossible to understand everything that had happened. But here she was, a witch, fleeing with Henry Lazar, who was either her former fiancé or a werewolf.

"Come on," Henry urged. "Peter's meeting us with horses in the alley." He still said the name as if it were something disgusting, something moldy in his mouth.

Of course! Her heart raced. Peter had not abandoned her after all. He would come for her, completing the action that Henry had begun.

She looked to Henry, racing through the night. An image flashed through her mind of the three of them on the run together, moving from town to town. She'd never have to choose.

Peter was meeting them. But wait. Henry had said, "I'm going to get you out of here." *I*, not *we*. Did he really want to help her still after she had spurned him?

They raced into Dye Makers Alley. Her fingers ached dully from clutching the knife under her cape as if she were wringing out a washrag. The shimmering vats of blue dye were there. The flower petals were there. But it was only after they'd reached the dead end that Valerie realized there were no horses.

"Where's Peter?" she heard herself ask.

"I don't know. He should be here by now. That was the plan." Henry looked huge, swelled up with anger.

It was just the two of them, alone in a dark, secluded place. The very place where yesterday the Wolf had told her she was his. And it had all come true; she was with him now.

All the pieces seemed to slide into place.

Peter was never coming, she thought.

Valerie felt drunk with the knowledge that she would die. She would put up one last fight; she wouldn't go easily. If she got him at just the right angle...maybe, just maybe... And as she thought it, there it was, his neck exposed as he leaned out over the vats to check the maw of the alley.

Probably checking for Solomon, making sure he'd have time to do his work well.

He had lured her sister into the night and murdered her, and he was trying to do the same to her. Well, *she* would not go easily.

Glancing up first at the red moon, Valerie raised her knife. She saw the blade shining in her hand, thirsty for blood. She was just stepping back so that she could throw her full weight into her blow when she froze.

There was a growl, both male and female, human and animal. The Devil's voice.

It was far away. Not in the alley.

"Oh my God. Henry."

He turned and saw her with the knife still raised.

He winced. "Could you put the blade back in your boot?" he asked, managing to ease the tension with a flash of his smile.

She sheepishly returned the knife to its place. Just then, another awful growl ripped through the air. Closer this time.

Valerie's relief was short-lived as a terrible new thought came over her.

"Henry, when was the last time you saw Peter?"

But Henry did not answer. Soldiers entered the alley, calling to each other, "The witch has escaped!"

He pulled her into one of the silos full of blue petals. Instantly they were wrapped in the sweet floral fragrance, strangely sweet when death was so near. Henry pushed her through the feathery mass, edging them toward the back wall.

"They're everywhere," he whispered.

Their bodies were wedged in close enough that they might touch but not close enough that they did. But then Valerie felt his hand on her waist, saw his eyes full of yearning. Her breath quickened. His hand slid down her leg. Why now?

She understood only when he'd gotten what he wanted.

The knife from her boot.

"Sorry," he said absently, an afterthought. His mind somewhere else, he hadn't even realized. He turned, preparing to ward off any assault, a gentleman always.

But she knew it would not be possible for them to defend themselves. There was no way. They would be caught within moments. All would be over.

But then Henry turned to her. "The church!"

He was right. The Wolf couldn't cross onto holy ground, and Father Solomon should respect its sanctuary as a priest himself. But they had to get there first....

Henry thought for a desperate moment, regarding the knife in his hand.

Moments later, Solomon's soldiers stormed the silo—finding only blue flower petals, some of them spilling out

into the street between the boards that had been pried
open.

Valerie and Henry had no choice but to run through the
openness of the square.

Somehow, over the noise of the soldiers searching the
town, the galloping of horses, the shouts of the villagers,
Valerie still heard the whisper.

"Valerie, where are you going?"

That eerie voice, a composite of all the voices she'd ever
known. Her heart leapt up into her throat, lodging itself
there. She knew before she looked. The Wolf had returned
for her.

She glanced at Henry, who had heard nothing. In the
periphery of her vision, a dark shape disappeared and
appeared again, bounding over roofs. It was only if she
looked out of the corner of her eye that she could be sure it
was still there.

They could see the church now. But behind them came
shouts, the sound of heavy boots in rapid pursuit.

An arrow whistled past them, close. Another, *closer.*

Valerie looked back—and screamed, seeing the silver
bolt flying straight and true, the one that was meant for
her, meant to end her life. Somehow, though, at the very
last moment, just when she should have felt the metal bury
deep inside her, she didn't.

Instead, she was jolted aside, and with a *thwap*, the bolt lodged itself in Henry's side. He'd taken it for her.

He jolted with the impact, and yet he was running so fast that it was a few pounding steps before he slowed.

It was in the left shoulder. It had missed his heart, seemed to have missed his lungs.

"Go, Valerie. Go." He shoved her with his good arm.

She had known him all her life, yet only now understood how good, how brave, how honorable, he was.

"No, Henry. I can't leave you."

She glanced back at the soldiers closing in.

But the church was so near.

She threw his good arm over her shoulder, and together they stumbled for the last dozen yards through the snow. As they held each other close, his blood stained her red cloak even darker.

They staggered up to the gates of the sanctuary. Two more steps... but Solomon stood in front of the gates marking holy ground, blocking the way.

"We claim sanctuary." Valerie threw the words at him.

"Oh, but you can't," Solomon replied, his voice razor sharp. "You're not on holy ground yet." He reached out and gripped the arrow in Henry's shoulder.

"And this belongs to me." He yanked the bolt from Henry's wound with a wet, fleshy *shlop*, the sound a spoon makes as it tears through watermelon.

Gritting his teeth against the pain, Henry staggered back

and clasped his other hand over his shoulder to try to stanch the bleeding.

Valerie wanted to peer inside the gaping wound, to know what was inside Henry that could radiate such goodness. It clicked into place, like fitting a key into a lock. They could have a happy life together, she knew all at once. It would be the best thing, for all of them.

Something heaved inside Valerie as she heard it again.

"Valerie."

She turned to face the Wolf. Its eyes glowing, like twin moons. Its lips glistening, wet and black.

Two soldiers lying dead at its feet.

The Wolf stood over her like a great monument. It was unmoving, the power of its shadow almost comforting.

Solomon's eyes darted up to the blood moon hanging low on the horizon, barely visible between the houses, its color paling.

With one decisive motion, he grabbed Valerie's yellow hair, jerking her neck back. He set his sword against her throat, using her as a human shield.

"We will stall. It's almost daybreak," he confided to the Captain in an abrupt whisper.

"You want her alive, don't you?" he called to the Wolf.

The Wolf glared at Solomon, then looked urgently at the fading moon, growing ever fainter in the sky.

Henry moved toward Valerie, but Solomon dug the

sword into her throat. Henry backed up. Valerie felt the edge of the blade sharp against her.

Inside the gate, she could see villagers edging closer to gawk, careful to stay on sacred ground, like children watching their parents argue from behind the stairwell rails. They'd run there in the commotion, no one willing to hunt the Wolf that they'd been so eager to slaughter only days before.

"First it dies, then you," Solomon whispered to Valerie, nodding to the masked bowman awaiting command from the bell tower, one arm resting carelessly atop the banister.

The bowman fired at the Wolf, but it jumped, sensing danger, and the bolt buried itself in the earth. Seeing the miss, Solomon reached his limit. He could not hold out any longer, bloodlust devouring him before the Wolf had a chance to. He threw Valerie free and charged full force at the Wolf, sword raised in readiness. The veins in his neck stood up like the branches of a tree grown enormous inside him from the seeds of his obsession.

But the Wolf leapt first, crunching its massive jaw onto Solomon's wrist, first through sinew, then through bone. The hand dropped heavily to the snowy ground, bitten clean off, its fearsome silver-tipped fingers still clenched around the hilt of the sword.

Moaning in agony, Solomon staggered backward toward the church, toward safety. The Wolf pursued him.

The masked bowman let loose with another rain of

arrows. Incensed, the Wolf swiped up one of the dead soldier's shields and sent it flying toward the bell tower. The disk slammed into the bowman's chest, splitting his armor, impaling him. He crashed into the bell, sending out a clang of doom.

Seizing the distraction, Henry grabbed Valerie and pulled her through the gateway onto sacred ground. The Wolf leapt forward, but they were already inside and it could not reach her.

The Wolf glanced again at the blood moon, already setting. The sky was showing the first hint of daylight as the buried sun unearthed itself.

The beast knew it had to act quickly. It reached its paw toward Valerie, over the stone threshold, but snatched it back as it started to catch fire. The Wolf snapped its teeth, glaring at its prey with all four of its eyes.

"**You can't hide from this.**" The Wolf's garbled voice had a strange lulling effect on Valerie. The Wolf would take care of her in a way she'd never been taken care of before. "**Step through the gate or I'll kill everyone. Do you understand?**"

"Yes, I understand," she said, almost in a trance.

"See how the witch talks to the Wolf!" Solomon sought vindication even in his crippled state, crying out from where a soldier was wrapping his wound.

"**Make your decision.**" The Wolf's voice echoed against the walls of her mind.

Valerie thought of all the people around her, of Henry.

She saw them, in all their flawed and perfect humanity. She couldn't let them die.

Time slowed for her. She was struck with the strangeness of existence. There was too much: too much beauty, too much love, too much pain and sorrow for one go-around. What to do with it all? Might it be better not to exist?

She stared back at the Wolf, weighing what it would mean to step forward. Those beautiful yellow eyes. Perhaps it would not be the worst thing.... And the idea became a fissure that widened inside her, like a crevice becoming a canyon. The solution was simple and dazzling. She felt there was some revenge in abandoning her will. The Wolf would not get Valerie, because she was not herself anymore.

She would let the Wolf take her.

She stepped toward the gate. It was surprisingly easy. She was just about to take the decisive step, the one that would bring her outside sacred ground, when Henry saw what she was doing and held her back, where the Wolf could not reach.

"I won't let you destroy my home. I'll go with you," Valerie said. "To save them." She felt her voice, high and false, coming from somewhere outside herself. She was not afraid of what would come next. She had decided. The world was not real to her anymore.

The stillness was deafening as the Wolf awaited her approach.

And then the spell was broken by a movement from the crowd behind her, from the very back. Someone coming, emerging, tripping over others' knees and satchels.

Roxanne.

Roxanne kept her head down as she moved forward. Valerie's heart skipped three beats seeing the beautiful sunset-colored hair. The Wolf she could bear. But not further accusations from those whom she had loved.

"I won't let you make that sacrifice." Roxanne stepped up beside her.

Valerie stared at her friend, not wanting to let herself believe. Roxanne gave her a brief nod, her eyes heavy with tears.

Rose stepped forward next. "Neither will I." She looked at Valerie with a deep flush in her cheeks, remembering how she had acted earlier, caught up in the fervor.

Marguerite, shamed by her own daughter's bravery, followed, as did other villagers, one by one: the tavern owner, the dye shop workers, woodcutters, friends of her father's. Prudence was the last to join them, but in the end she, too, stepped forward, fighting her own bitter emotions.

Daggorhorn felt it was lifting into flight, a flock finding its wings together.

The town's people, emerging from its nightmare, held to one another, raising a barrier against the Wolf. But it was also a barrier against the evil they had allowed into themselves. For a few moments, the center of the universe was right there, in the village churchyard.

315

The Wolf had not planned for this. It growled, furious, so close to what it wanted and yet unable to reach her.

The moon had disappeared from the sky. Morning had come, and the Wolf knew it could not stay or it would be revealed in human form. Its eyes blazed at Valerie for one last moment, then, with an enraged snarl, it charged into the night.

The villagers exhaled, afraid to look at each other, to break the spell. But they did, and still the Wolf was gone. They had done what was right, and they had done it together.

Only Valerie saw Solomon coming toward her, worse than the beast itself, ungovernable rage lining his face, ready to claim the vengeance he felt he'd earned. His one hand was held out, and Valerie reached out to protect herself. But he went for her head, cupping his hand, forcing all his weight into it, slamming her skull down against the stone wall. A ripple of shock passed through the shattered villagers.

Solomon clutched her by the hair and raised her face to meet his. "You will still burn, witch."

Henry charged, and Solomon whipped around, ready to slash with his remaining nails.

But a bullwhip came first, whistling elegantly through the air, attaching itself to Solomon and jerking his arm back. Shocked, Solomon looked around and saw the Captain approaching, hard-faced.

"Under the blood moon, a man bitten is a man cursed," the hulking Captain reminded his commander.

Solomon did not flinch at the truth. Still, he could not help saying, "My children will be orphans."

"My brother had children, too," the Captain sneered.

Father Solomon looked down at his arm, letting it sink in that the corruption was growing within him. He was no better than the Wolf he had hunted. He was a man true to his convictions, true to them to the bitterest of ends. He believed in purity and in purification; in the cold, unsentimental elimination of evil.

With his remaining hand, he made the sign of the cross.

"Forgive your lost sheep, Father. I meant only to serve you, to protect us from darkness..." he started but did not finish.

The Captain, who believed in revenge, too, swung his sword. Sharpened to something beyond a razor's edge, it pierced quickly and cleanly through Solomon's heart, without catching at the bone, just as Solomon had killed the Captain's brother.

Roxanne looked away, but Valerie didn't. An evil had been dealt with, one among many. She felt something on her temple. Blood trickling from the wound where Solomon had hit her head against the wall.

Just seeing it, wet on her fingers, made dizziness come over her. She sank to her knees.

Where is Peter? she wondered again.

Then the world became a nowhere place and lost its grounding. She fell down, down, deep into the center of everything.

29

Valerie reentered the world from a place of darkness. She looked around, recognizing the blanket. Grandmother's. But hadn't it once been white? Now it was red, the red of her cape. Vibrant, like something alive.

Soft snow had begun to fall again, forming huge, pillowy banks outside, as it never had before. It must have snowed all night. The sky was flat and white, like a dream. Valerie looked over at the shape next to her. Grandmother. It should have been Lucie. Where was Lucie? Gone. She would always be gone, as though she had never existed at all.

Valerie's waking seemed to have woken up Grandmother, too. She rolled over to face Valerie and opened her eyes.

They were wet and globular, her pupils expanded. Round like marbles.

"What big eyes you have, Grandmother," Valerie noted calmly. She saw that every feature of Grandmother's face was defined and accentuated. Valerie felt the way she felt when she drank too much water too fast, empty and full and dizzy.

"The better to see you with, my dear," Grandmother said in a low muffle.

Her ears, too, were peeking out from beneath her tousled hair, strangely pointed.

"What big ears you have, Grandmother."

"The better to hear you with, my dear."

As Grandmother spoke these last words, she revealed at last her teeth—oh, her teeth. They looked longer and sharper than usual.

"What big teeth you have, Grandmother."

"The better to eat you with, my dear...."

Grandmother lunged—

Valerie started awake with a strangled cry. Orienting herself, she found she was in her own bed, Roxanne lying asleep beside her, the morning light spilling across her face. Catching her breath, Valerie stared at her friend.

Roxanne was not Lucie, either.

Suzette, who had been beside the bed watching Valerie sleep, leaned down over her.

"Darling," she began in a sweet voice that was foreign to Valerie. She had a faraway look in her eyes. Valerie looked at the deep wound marring her mother's face; could it be infected? She looked around, and everything seemed strange, not as it should have been. Objects seemed dreamlike, too big, too small.

"I've made you some porridge, your favorite," her mother said in the same sweet drone. Valerie breathed in. The smell of molasses was overpowering. She bit her lip. *Am I awake?* It was hard to tell anymore.

Suzette's face was set in an unnatural smile. Valerie ducked under her mother's arm and moved down the ladder barefoot, two rungs at a time.

"Valerie?" her mother questioned, her head cocked to one side, like a little girl putting on an act.

"I'm leaving now," Valerie replied, pulling on her boots, gathering a handkerchief and some fruit for her basket and settling her scarlet cloak around her shoulders. Roxanne stirred in bed, opening her eyes, wiping her nose.

"Leaving?" Suzette asked, amused. "Where to, darling?"

"To Grandmother's. I had...I think she might be in danger." She also needed to find Peter, if he was somewhere to be found. And Henry.

"Oh, Valerie. You don't always need to take care of everyone. I made porridge, your favorite," Suzette repeated, resting her hand on Valerie's cheek. Her hand felt clammy and cold. Reptilian. Valerie looked up at her mother.

"You're safe with us," she whispered. Roxanne peered down from the loft, her covers pulled up to her chin, blinking awake, unsure of what to make of the scene.

"Good-bye, Mother, Roxanne." Valerie felt solitary, whole unto herself. She needed no one.

Valerie was met with the sting of the cold as she stepped out the door. It felt right, somehow. She needed a shock of something. She needed to know she was alive.

She tightened her cloak around her, slipped the hood up over her head. The blustering wind swept across her body, blowing into her cloak, inflating it with icy air. She held her basket in front of her, her fingers clutching the wicker handle. Windswept ice crystals lodged between the wicker strands.

No one was around.

As she walked through the village, the snow did not remember where she had been, her footprints neatly erased by more as the flakes fell in a thick blanket. She passed the brazen elephant, lying on its side, hacked open. *Had someone been in there?* Valerie shivered, thinking of Claude, of the cruelty she'd learned humanity was capable of. She was disgusted; perhaps it would be better to be a beast than a human.

The world of winter meant that people stayed inside. When a storm like this descended, it was impossible to know what lay around bends, what was kept hidden behind or ahead.

Someone came into view then. Valerie saw that it was Henry, saddling a beautiful steed, adjusting the stirrups. She warmed at the sight of him.

The Captain motioned to the soldiers, who were suiting up, and they retreated as she came near, perhaps out of respect for privacy but maybe out of mistrust.

"Valerie."

The horse shifted, venting steam from its nostrils into the winter morning air, anxious to go, as though it were in the presence of something evil.

"Easy," Henry quieted it. He looked proud. Dutiful. He had found a new calling. He would go after the Wolf. Good replacing evil, she hoped.

"You're a warrior," she said, her green eyes electrified.

"You are, too," he replied.

Valerie wrapped her arms around him, standing on her toes to reach his neck with her lips. Gently, they found skin, which was soft and warm. It felt like something that would melt if it sat out for too long in the sun. It thrilled her.

She felt the smooth of Henry's hand against her cheek. And then their bodies pulled apart, making a clean break.

He hesitated, running a hand through his light brown hair.

"What is it?" she asked.

"No one has seen Peter, Valerie," he said, hoisting himself into the saddle. "And when I find him... I'll do what I have to." She felt the vastness of his shape atop the horse,

325

and then he was gone, riding into the blank slate of wilderness, the great warrior.

Valerie felt indebted to him, for so many things. She had chosen evil over good, and he had stood by her, sacrificing himself to protect her from the Wolf, to save her from herself. She had broken Henry's heart, for the love of Peter— someone who had always taken without asking. How had she not seen how steady and secure things could have been with Henry? She felt calm in her new understanding.

With each stride of Henry's galloping steed, Valerie, who'd never needed anyone, felt a tiny hollow open and expand within herself.

Valerie ran, her feet alternately sinking in the snow and finding the brittle surface of the winter ground, her legs working smoothly, mechanically, moving her through the storm. She felt sure that something was very wrong at Grandmother's... not that much was right anymore. Something was happening, something dark, and she had to be there because she did not have the strength to stay away.

She did not stop in the field to think of Lucie, or in the grove to think of Claude. Her heart did not flutter as she passed the Great Pine. Her losses, her past. The places were indistinguishable in the leveling white. She didn't stop to find her bearings but rather let herself be carried by the momentum of urgency.

She passed the river, frozen over into a smooth top, like a bowl of milk. She heard the surface crackle as a branch was felled.

Finally, she came to the Black Raven Woods. She was not far from the tree house, a hundred yards, but the path she'd taken so many times now seemed endless. She was still light-headed from her injury, and the bleached world around her moved in and out of focus. The only sounds she heard were the gusts whistling through the frozen branches.

She glanced around. Nothing in the brush. Nothing ahead but where she was going, nothing behind but where she'd been. Clean sheets of snow were being blown to the ground by the second. Valerie moved forward, her knuckles white now from gripping the basket, the suede of her boots soaked through with cold. The hood of her long red cloak framed her pale face, her pink cheeks.

Instinctively, she knew just where to set each foot, having followed the route so many times. And yet she felt she was working too hard to move forward, as if she were swimming through oil. The air sliced through her, crisp and still, and the gray of the sky was scribbled with tree branches. There was an absence of scent; even her senses were frozen. In the cold, fingers were unfeeling, eyes were unseeing.

The snow began falling so thickly that anything farther than five feet in front of her was lost to the blooming white. She was not sure she was conscious. Valerie could feel the barely audible hum in the trees. Now and then something cracked, but when she looked, there was nothing.

And yet she could *feel* something behind her, approaching. She sharpened her hearing, tried to be silent even as she picked up her pace to a run. *An animal.* Surely it was an animal. *Daylight*, she reminded herself. *Can't be the Wolf.*

Yes. Something was there. She was sure.

She heard it, louder. And louder.

Closer.

She slowed. She was not afraid, she told herself. It could be Suzette running after her, upset about the way she left the house. Or Henry, to tell her he would stay.

But . . . it *could* be the Wolf in its human form. Whatever it was, she decided, it could not be more awful than what she'd already confronted. She turned, beaten, ready to face a dark fate.

What she saw made her stomach lurch, almost brought her to her knees.

The dark apparition emerging from the snow brought her back to life, yanked her out of her surrender. She staggered backward a few steps but could move no farther.

It was Peter, *her* Peter, stalking after the girl he loved, the girl he could not live without. His black shirt was torn, his cloak missing.

"Valerie, thank God you're all right."

His face was glistening with cold. He was beautiful, the

snow in his eyelashes like diamonds, the cool pink of his cheeks, the wet red of his lips. He was staggering toward her.

"I have to leave you." His breath came in uneven bursts. "You won't be safe with me."

Whatever he was, he could not be bad. An amazing and terrible thought entered Valerie's mind, clearing away all others.

"Peter..."

She stepped toward him, arms out. They gave in to each other, finally, their bodies fitting together. Her cold fingers warmed on his cheek, and his arms slipped underneath her crimson cloak as her long blond hair blew around them. Enveloped in a shelter of white, standing out in black and red, were just the two of them. Nothing else anywhere. Valerie knew that she could never be apart from him, that she was what he was and that she would be his always.

She didn't care if he was the Wolf or not. And if he was a Wolf, then she would be one, too.

She made her choice and brought her lips to his.

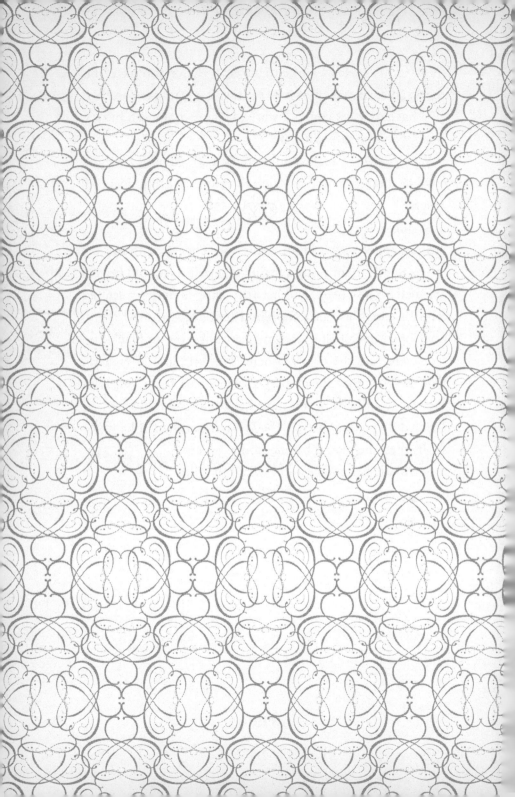

Is this truly
the end of
Valerie's story?

Visit
www.redridinghoodbook.com
to find out.

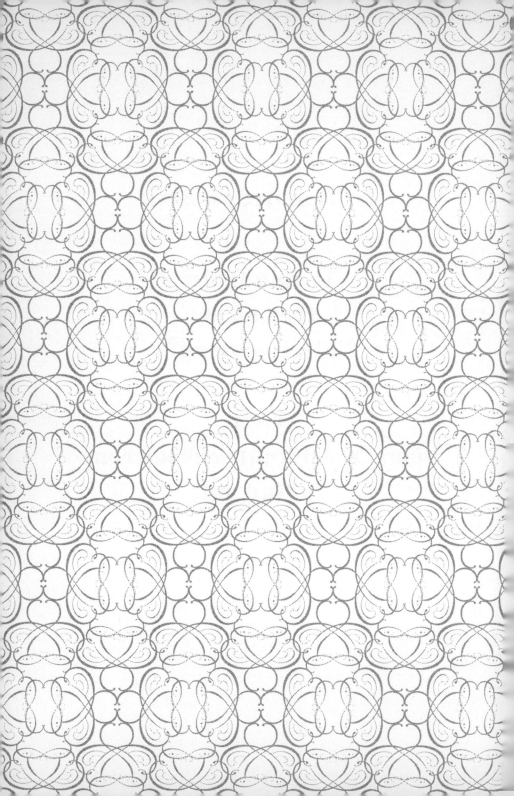

Acknowledgments

I would like to thank DAVID LESLIE JOHNSON AND CATHERINE HARDWICKE for creating magic.

JENNIFER DAVISSON KILLORAN, JULIE YORN, MICHAEL IRELAND, ALEX MACE, AND THE WARNER BROS. TEAM for their unswerving support.

MARCUS ANDERSSON, NIKKI RAMEY, PATRICK SANCHEZ-SMITH, AND ADRIANA STIMOLA for their encouragement and patience through the many drafts.

As always, I am indebted to CARROLL CARTWRIGHT AND MARY GORDON, who've taught me everything.

I would also especially like to thank ERIN STEIN, MY EDITOR AT LITTLE, BROWN, for taking a leap of faith and for being such a phenomenal guide.

Sarah Blakley-Cartwright is a recent cum laude graduate of Barnard College. She is a recipient of the 2008–2009 Mary Gordon Fiction Scholarship Award and the 2009–2010 Lenore Marshall Barnard Prize for Prose. She grew up in Los Angeles and Mexico. She now writes in New York City and Los Angeles. Despite what the book may say, she actually prefers wolves to people.

David Leslie Johnson

Raised in Mansfield, Ohio, **David Leslie Johnson** began writing plays in the second grade and wrote his first screenplay at age nineteen. He graduated from the Ohio State University in Columbus with a bachelor of fine arts degree in photography and cinema. After working as a production assistant on the Academy Award–nominated film *The Shawshank Redemption*, Johnson spent five years as an assistant to the film's director and writer, Frank Darabont, learning the trade of screenwriting from one of the industry's most respected talents.

Johnson's most recent project was writing an original screenplay for the film *Red Riding Hood*, directed by Catherine Hardwicke. He currently has several projects in development. Johnson lives in Burbank, California, with his wife, screenwriter Kimberly Lofstrom Johnson, and their son, Samuel.

Matt Holyoak

Catherine Hardwicke worked in film production design before she became an award-winning director for the films *Thirteen*, *Lords of Dogtown*, and *The Nativity Story* and the international blockbuster *Twilight*, based on the novel by Stephenie Meyer. Hardwicke's films have garnered dozens of accolades, including Academy Award and Golden Globe nominations and six MTV Movie Awards.

Hardwicke is also the author of the *New York Times* bestseller *Twilight: Director's Notebook*. Her most recent project is a dark, Gothic adaptation of "Red Riding Hood."